ENDURANCE SERIES

WORKBOOK

The Endurance Series Workbook can be used as a self-paced module that allows for flexibility in learning styles.

Designed for advanced middle grade to high school learners, this workbook is a companion to the historical fiction graphic novel series, *Endurance, Book One: The Frozen Keep* and *Book Two: The Beckoning Shore.* The graphic novel chronicles Sir Ernest Shackleton's quest to cross Antarctica in the years 1914-1916.

This guide has a wide range of topics that are easy to follow and understand. You will discover what a member of the Trans-Antarctic expedition would need to master for survival: common sense, logic, map reading, decision making and problem solving. The story illuminates important qualities of human character, whether it be honesty, integrity, and self-sacrifice, or the darker sides of fear, greed, and anger.

The questions in this workbook are designed to cover different levels of learning, from simple knowledge questions to in-depth evaluations of what students have read. You'll find two types of questions:

Low-level questions: These ask students to recall facts, understand basic ideas, and apply those facts and ideas to different situations. These are simpler questions that help students build their knowledge.

High-level questions: *Marked with a ship's scout icon.* Students use their new-found knowledge to analyze the differences and similarities in ideas, evaluate and judge ideas, and create something new from the information they've gathered. These questions may require students to research and gather additional information, so make sure that internet access is available to them.

My hope is that you enjoy the adventure, and also learn more about the world in which we live!

The Endurance Series Workbook

Written and illustrated by Terrill Sullivan

Edited by Adelé Hensley, Certified Editor in the Life Sciences (ELS)

Special thanks to **Gary D. Soto** for his sage wisdom and advice in actively helping this workbook meet the educational requirements of high school learners. **He is a recipient of the National Educator Award for Reshaping American Education.**

Proofreaders: Gayle Gustafson, Rosanne Plant

Shackleton quotes are from *South* by Sir Ernest Henry Shackleton, New York: Macmillan, 1920

Worsley quotes are from: *Endurance: an Epic of Polar Adventure*, by Frank Arthur Worsley, London: P. Allan & co., 1931

Compass Vectors by vecteezy.com. Pirate icon created by max.icons - Flaticon

Images of *Endurance22* expedition courtesy Falklands Maritime Heritage Trust

The Endurance Series Workbook © 2024 Terrill Sullivan

ISBN 979-8-218-46801-9

Library of Congress Control Number: 2024917648

Printed in the USA

Terrill Sullivan
High Tide Editions
Carlsbad, California
www.terrillsullivan.com

PREFACE

The early 20th century marked the end of the European Age
of Discovery, with the last act being the Heroic Age of Polar Exploration.
It was a period of fundamental change, as the Western World was transformed
during the Industrial Age by breakthroughs in manufacturing, transportation,
housing and agriculture that we still benefit from in this present age. But on the
dark side, it also brought the advent of mechanized warfare into World War I,
and led to the unforeseen destruction of ecosystems that have
affected us to this day.

ELA, History-Social Science, and Science for High School with SBAC and NGSS Alignment

This workbook integrate ELA, history-social science, and science standards relevant to high school-level learning objectives. The questions align with specific **Smarter Balanced Assessment Consortium (SBAC) standards** in both Mathematics and English Language Arts/Literacy (ELA/Literacy), as well as incorporating elements from the **Next Generation Science Standards (NGSS),** which are often integrated into SBAC assessments. Here's how they match:

English Language Arts (ELA)

Vocabulary Acquisition and Use
Grades 9-10: Determine or clarify the meaning of unknown and multiple-meaning words and phrases (L.9-10.4).
Grades 11-12: Same as above but at an advanced level (L.11-12.4).

Literary and Textual Analysis
Literary Analysis: Analyze the cumulative impact of specific word choices on meaning and tone, including personification (RL.9-10.4, RL.11-12.4).
Textual Analysis and Interpretation: Determine a theme or central idea of a text and analyze its development (RL.9-10.2, RL.11-12.2).Analyze how plot and characters develop and how themes are conveyed (RL.9-10.3, RL.11-12.3).

Textual Evidence and Inference
Reading Informational Texts: Cite strong and thorough textual evidence to support analysis of content and inferences (RI.9-10.1, RI.11-12.1). Analyze how authors unfold an analysis or series of ideas, including the order and connections (RI.9-10.3, RI.11-12.3).
Literary Texts: Determine the meaning of words and phrases, including figurative and connotative meanings (RL.9-10.4, RL.11-12.4).

Research and Synthesis
Research Projects: Conduct short and sustained research projects to answer questions or solve problems, using multiple sources (W.9-10.7, W.11-12.7).

Writing
Informative/Explanatory Texts: Examine and convey complex ideas clearly through effective selection, organization, and analysis (W.9-10.2, W.11-12.2).
Argumentative Writing: Write arguments to support claims using valid reasoning and sufficient evidence (W.9-10.1, W.11-12.1).

Character Analysis and Motivation
Analyze complex characters' development, interactions, and contributions to the plot and theme (RL.9-10.3, RL.11-12.3).

History-Social Science

Historical Context and Analysis
Analyze causes and impacts of significant historical events, such as World War I, technological advancements in the 20th century, and significant movements (HSS.10.5, HSS.11.5, HSS.11.7).

Geography and Geographical Skills
Analyze social, economic, and political issues with geographical context (HSS.11.11).Use geographic tools to analyze spatial organization (HSS.10.10).

Historical Research and Inquiry
Understand the role of industrialization, technological advancements, and geographical factors in historical exploration (HSS.11.3, HSS.10.4, HSS.10.10).

Science (NGSS) Integrated with SBAC

Scientific Inquiry and Application
Use mathematical or computational representations to predict planetary motions (HS-ESS1-4).

Environmental Science
Evaluate or refine technological solutions to reduce environmental impacts (HS-ESS3-4).

Engineering and Technology
Analyze global challenges using qualitative and quantitative criteria (HS-ETS1-1).Create solutions to complex problems by breaking them down (HS-ETS1-2).Analyze complex problems by specifying criteria and constraints (HS-ETS1-3).

Earth and Space Science
Plan and conduct investigations on properties of water, climate changes, and carbon cycling (HS-ESS2-1, HS-ESS2-4, HS-ESS2-5, HS-ESS2-6).

Biology and Ecosystems
Develop models for hierarchical systems in organisms, and evaluate interactions in ecosystems (HS-LS1-2, HS-LS2-6, HS-LS2-8).

Physical Science
Use mathematical representations to support claims about physical systems and forces (HS-PS1-4, HS-PS3-4, HS-PS2-4).

Cross-Disciplinary

Research and Synthesis
Conduct research projects to solve problems or answer questions, synthesizing multiple sources (W.9-10.7, W.11-12.7).

Historical and Cultural Understanding
Analyze how authors transform source material in their works (RL.9-10.9, RL.11-12.9).

Language and Expression
Demonstrate understanding of figurative language, word relationships, and nuances (L.9-10.5, L.11-12.5).

Critical Thinking
Synthesize information from multiple sources to solve problems (RST.9-10.7, RST.11-12.7).

Math & Engineering
Analyze global challenges with qualitative and quantitative criteria (HS-ETS1-1).

Sources & Recommendations

South

Author: **Sir Ernest Shackleton**

The official journal of the British Imperial Trans-Antarctic Expedition. Very detailed account with amazing descriptions of the environment they encountered.

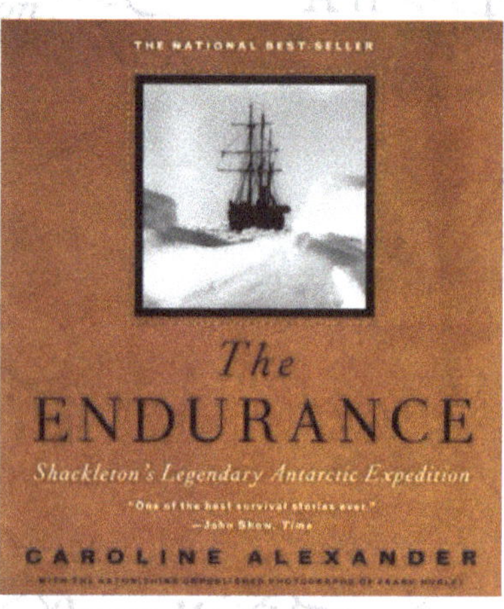

The Endurance: Shackleton's Legendary Antarctic Expedition

Author: **Caroline Alexander**

This well written account is difficult to put down. Inserted throughout are the legendary photographs of Frank Hurley which adds to this authentic retelling. A bestseller in its initial release.

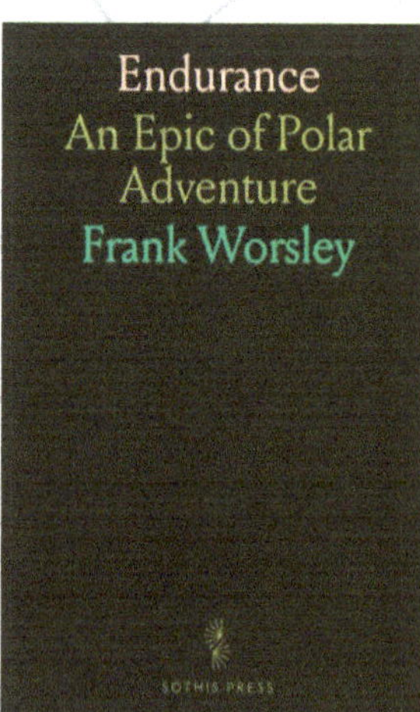

Endurance: ***An Epic of Polar Adventure***

Author: **Frank Worsley**
Captain and navigator on the *Endurance* ship. First person account of the events.

Endurance: Shackleton's Incredible Voyage

Author: **Alfred Lansing**

"One of the best adventure books ever written" (Wall Street Journal). A New York Times bestseller.

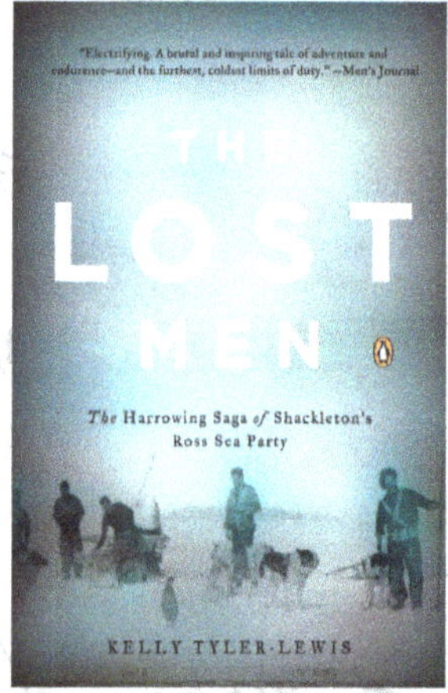

The Lost Men: The Harrowing Saga of Shackleton's Ross Sea Party

Author: **Kelly Tyler-Lewis**

A gripping account of the tragic Ross Sea Party– Shackleton's relief team for his epic crossing of the Antarctic continent.

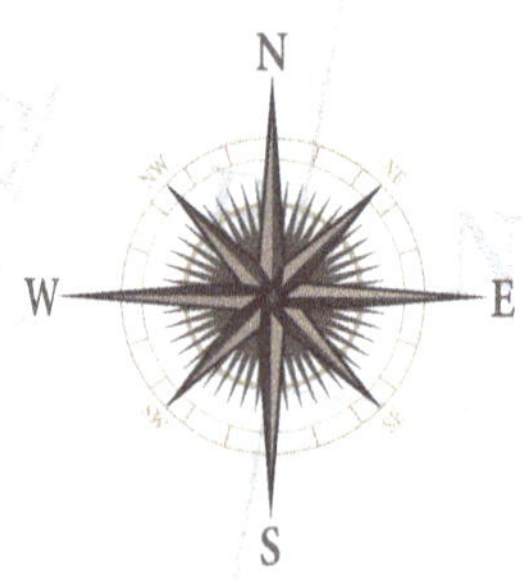

TABLE OF CONTENTS

Commander of the 1914 Imperial Trans-Antarctic Expedition.

Young electrician hired on the expedition through the help of his brother Edward.

Daughter of a merchant on the Island of South Georgia. Falls in love with Jack.

Veteran Antarctic explorer. Second-in-Command of the expedition.

Jack's friend. Shipwrecked in Argentina, he sneaked on board the *Endurance*.

Jack's brother. Left the expedition to fight for Britain in World War I.

Captain of the *Endurance* and navigator for the expedition.

Able-bodied seaman hired to maintain the sails and rigging of the *Endurance*.

Veteran Antarctic explorer. One of Shackleton's trusted men.

Book One, THE FROZEN KEEP

1. Define "keep" as both a verb and a noun.

Noun: ______________________________

Verb: ______________________________

2. Explain how the title *The Frozen Keep* acts as a metaphor for the *Endurance* ship. What implications does this metaphor have for Shackleton and his crew?

____

____

INTRODUCTION / PROLOGUE

3. Summarize the primary objective of the *Endurance* expedition of 1914.

____

____

4. Describe the historical context of the *Endurance's* departure and its significance.

____

____

5. Describe the sensory experiences Leah Carlberg encounters upon arriving at the Grytviken whaling station on the Island of South Georgia.

____

____

6. One of the themes throughout the book is regret. What does Leah regret?

____

____

7. Analyze Leah's reaction to the sight of the industry and factories on the Island of South Georgia. What decision does she make?

____

____

The Hunt

8. The projectile used to hunt whales is a harpoon. Comparing a hand-thrown harpoon to a cannon harpoon, how does the use of a cannon harpoon affect the number of whales caught compared to a hand-thrown one?

____

____

____

____

____

____

The *Endurance* Nears the Island of South Georgia

Below deck, the captain is consulting with Ernest Shackleton, the leader of the expedition, about their voyage. They are looking over their progress so far and how to best navigate to the island.

9. Plotting a sea voyage is called

_______________________ a course.

The *Endurance* left England and arrived in Buenos Aires, Argentina before sailing on to South Georgia.

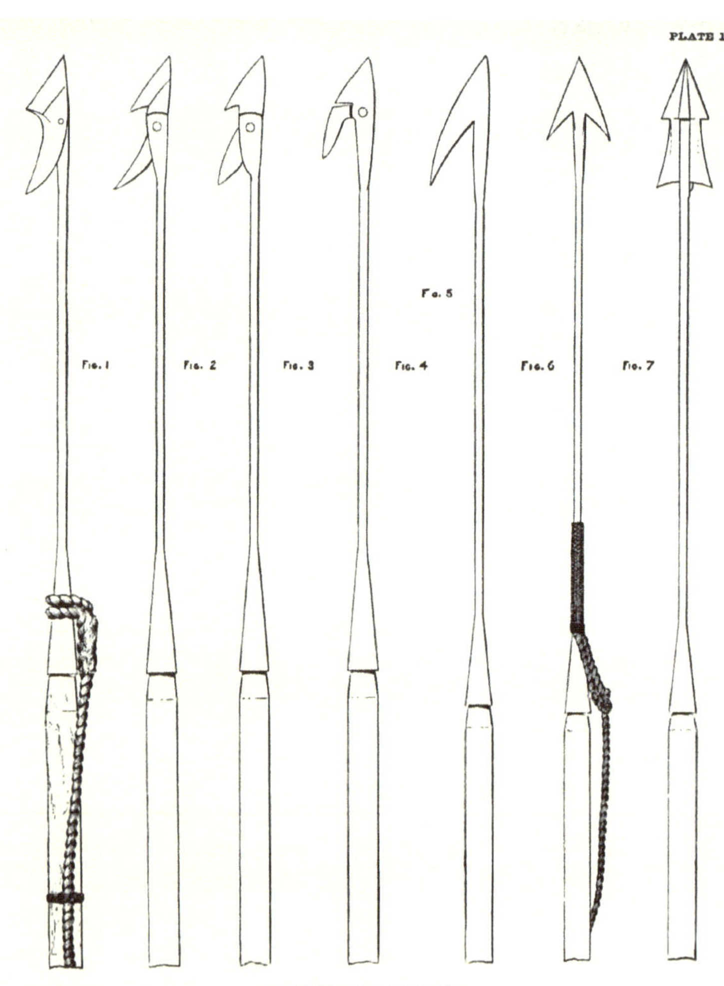

THE WHALE FISHERY.

Harpoons. (Sect. v, vol. ii, p. 250.)

FIG. 1. Improved harpoon or toggle-iron now in general use.
FIGS. 2, 3. First forms of toggle-irons made by Lewis Temple.
FIG. 4. "One-flued" harpoon with hinged toggle.
FIG. 5. "One-flued" harpoon.
FIG. 6. "Two-flued" harpoon.
FIG. 7. Provincetown toggle-iron; not now in use.

Image courtesy of U.S. National Oceanic and Atmospheric Administration

10. Explain why the explorers used a ship instead of an airplane for their journey. When was the first flight to Antarctica?

Grytviken, South Georgia

The grimy factory town greeted the arrival of the *Endurance* as big news.

11. Using the map below, mark and label where Grytviken is located on the Island of South Georgia.

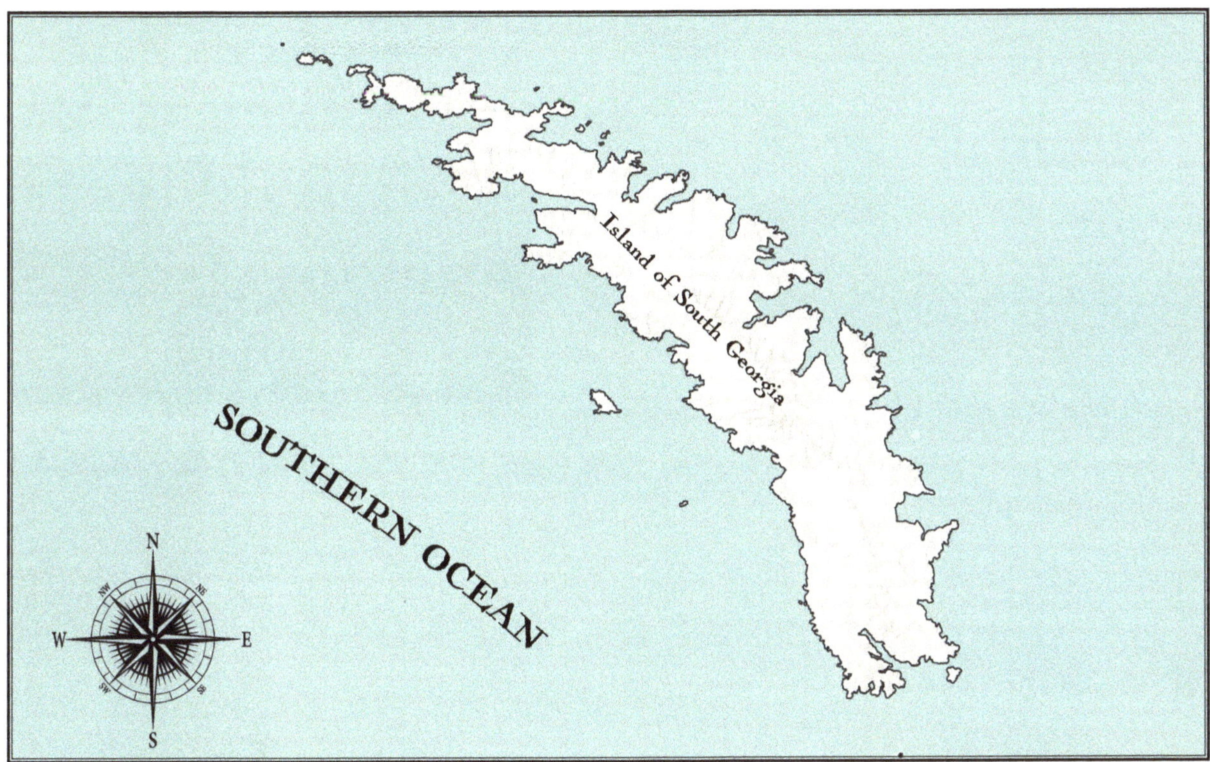

CHAPTER 1 | A FAR COUNTRY

12. On a cold afternoon, Jack Robinson and Perce Blackborow survey the aftermath of a bloody harvest. Discuss their observations and the major event occurring in Europe in the fall of 1914.

13. Investigate and explain the connection between the demand for whales and World War I.

14. Why did Jack's brother, Edward, quit the expedition?

15. List the responsibilities an electrician would have on a ship in 1914.

16. Discuss why Frank Wild is upset with the German whaling captain and his crew.

Leah Makes Her Entrance

17. Leah enters the tavern feeling frustrated and depressed. What are her reasons?

18. Analyze the hidden motive behind the Germans harassing Leah.

19. When Jack intervenes, the German captain challenges him, leading Frank Wild to step in. What does the German captain imply by his insult of Frank?

20. Define foreshadowing. How is Frank's response a form of foreshadowing?

21. Many of the men—including Jack—seem to think that fighting in the war is the ultimate form of bravery. But how are the crew of the *Endurance* also showing bravery?

22. The mix of people on South Georgia in 1914 could have led to an explosive situation since they were on opposite sides of World War I. And it eventually did—the Hope Bay incident, the Deception Island incident, and the Falklands War. Choose one of these three conflicts to research, and write a paragraph that includes the year of the conflict, the parties involved, and the reasons for the conflict.

23. Research and summarize the Antarctic Treaty. Explain its significance to international relations. Why is it important in light of the conflicts above? **Enter the date it was signed in the timeline on page 37.**

Jack Finds Leah

Jack then hurries off to a rendezvous he's been dreading. Meeting Leah on this desolate island was beyond his wildest dreams, but now he will have to say goodbye...

24. Describe Leah's reaction to Jack finding her on the mountain. Analyze why she was angry about being discovered.

25. Jack, desperate to find a way out of this predicament, offers to stay on South Georgia and work as a whaler. What is Leah's response?

"It doesn't matter...You'll leave and I'll never see ya again... The old whalers say you will all die on the ice like Scott did..."

26. Research Robert Falcon Scott's 1912 Antarctic expedition and compare it with Shackleton's. Describe some key differences between their expeditions.

27. Leah mentions that her parents want her to marry Svensen, a whaler from the factory. Jack reacts emotionally: *You hate that he kills whales!* What is Leah trying to provoke within Jack? What does Leah say in response to Jack's outburst?

28. When Leah and Jack make their way down off the mountain, they enter Grytviken. Research the uses of whale oil in the early 20th century. Explain its significance and applications during that time period.

____

____

____

____

29. What substitute for whale oil do we use today?

____

____

30. **Add the date Grytviken was established to page 37.** Investigate the current status of Grytviken. Analyze factors contributing to its current status, including environmental concerns and international regulations.

____

____

____

____

____

The Flensing Plan, Grytviken, South Georgia. Image by expedition photographer Frank Hurley, November 1915. Taken while the *Endurance* was docked in Grytviken before they sailed to the Weddell Sea.

Rusted and abandoned whaling ships, Grytviken. Photograph by Liam Quinn

31. Explain how whalers in the early 20th century used parts of whales such as blubber, meat, bones, and viscera. Discuss the economic and practical purposes of each.

Blubber: ____

____

Meat: ____

____

Bones: ____

____

Viscera: ____

____

32. Research and describe international efforts to protect whales. Discuss one specific conservation measure or treaty aimed at preserving whale populations.

33. On the dock, Jack and Leah say a painful goodbye. Based on Leah's final words to Jack, analyze her feelings about Shackleton's expedition and its impact on her.

34. That night in Grytviken, the Southern Lights appear. Describe their scientific nature and explain why they are visible only at the Earth's poles.

Perce's story

In the morning, Perce Blackborow and Jack arrive on deck to find Shackleton ready to depart for Antarctica. As they wait, Perce reminisces how he came to be a part of the expedition: *I'm so lucky to be here... Being stuck in Buenos Aires from a shipwreck...*

35. Buenos Aires is the capital of which nation?

36. What's the term for someone who sneaks aboard a ship for free passage?

37. Based on their experiences, analyze what Leah, Jack, and Perce are seeking in life. Compare their motivations and aspirations.

____

____

____

____

Shackleton Addresses the Crew

38. How did the public respond to Shackleton's expedition plans? Describe the number of applicants and how many were chosen for the expedition.

____

____

39. _I am aware of the criticism we received…_Examine the criticisms Shackleton faced regarding his expedition plans.

____

____

____

____

40. What day did England enter the war? _______________________
Add to the timeline on page 37.

41. What did the Expedition agree to do for the war effort and what was the Admiralty's response?

____

____

____

42. How were whaling ships used during WW1? Research online to find the answer.

____

____

____

43. Conduct research to identify and list five significant contributions or achievements of Winston Churchill:

1.____

____

2.____

____

3.____

____

4.____

____

5.____

Preparing to Sail

44. What was the official name of Shackleton's expedition?

____

45. This voyage will test the _Endurance_ to her limits. How will it also test the men?

____

46. _"Get ready for making sail! Crean! Rig the capstan!"_ What is the **capstan**?

____

47. Discuss the reasons why ships like the *Endurance* might require multiple anchors. Explain the advantages of having multiple anchors in various maritime situations.

48. Identify where the *Endurance* was built and describe the materials used in her construction. Discuss the significance of these details for the expedition.

49. Explain why the Heroic Age of Polar Exploration occurred during the Industrial Age. Analyze how technological advancements of the time influenced polar expeditions.

50. When did the *Endurance* depart Grytviken? _________________________ **Add to page 37.**

51. What does Wild say we must do to earn the trust of men?

52. How does the ship's name *Endurance* compare with Frank's admonishment for Jack to "Finish the course."?

CHAPTER 2 | THE MEASURE OF A MAN

1. Remembering the cliff incident in Grytviken, what fear is gripping Jack aloft? Discuss how fear impacts decision-making and relationships within the crew.

2. Determine responsibility for the knife incident. Analyze the consequences of such incidents in isolated environments like aboard the *Endurance*.

3. Based on Shackleton and Worsley's conversation, chart the *Endurance* course from Grytviken to Vahsel Bay by drawing a dashed line.

4. Shackleton compared their 20th century trek to the earlier European Age of Exploration. Describe 3 significant explorers and what they discovered from that era.

5. Shackleton tried to reach the South Pole _________ times. What happened the first two times?

____

____

____

____

6. Who was the first to reach the South Pole? What country was he from? **Add the date they arrived at the pole to the timeline on page 37.**

____

7. Explain why the explorer who first reached the South Pole succeeded where others had failed. Discuss the factors contributing to his achievement.

____

____

____

8. Describe what happened to Robert Falcon Scott's team on their attempt to reach the South Pole in 1910. **Add the date Scott and his party perished to page 37.**

____

____

____

____

9. Describe what the **Trans Continental Party** was to do for the expedition.

____

____

____

10. Describe what the **Ross Sea Party** was to do.

____

____

____

11. List synonyms or related terms for the word 'sledge' as used in polar exploration. Discuss the significance of sledges (sleds) in Antarctic expeditions.

More Troubles for Jack

12. When two dogs begin to fight, Jack intervenes trying to stop them, and is bitten. What should Jack have done? Check the answers below you think would be best.

    ☐ He did the right thing, but should be more careful.

    ☐ Yell and throw water on them to stop.

    ☐ Use a board to separate them and call for help.

    ☐ Kick one of the dogs or hit them with a stick.

13. Marlow won't stop bullying Jack, causing rage and anxiety within him. What advice could a man like Frank Wild or Shackleton give to young men like Jack and Perce in this situation?

14. **Fear and doubt begin to plague Shackleton.**
    Personification is the representation of a thing or idea as a person, such as Jack Frost representing winter. What is the Grim Reaper personifying?

15. Contrast how Jack and Shackleton deal with fear and doubt differently.

16. Tom Crean spots pack ice off the port bow. What side of the ship is that? _________________. What is the opposite side called in nautical terms? _________________.

17. On December 7, 1914, the *Endurance* enters the pack ice of the Weddell Sea. **Enter the date on page 37.**

The *Endurance*

18. Originally named *Polaris*, she was launched December 17, 1912 at Framnæs shipyard in Norway. When one of her owners went bankrupt, she was bought by Shackleton in January 1914. The expedition would be her first voyage. **Add both dates to page 37.**

19. Using the blueprint of the *Polaris* below, investigate online to label these parts of the ship from this list:

Spanker   Main Gaff   Crow's Nest   Bowsprit   Hull   Flying Jib   Foremast   Topgallant Sail   Topsail Yard

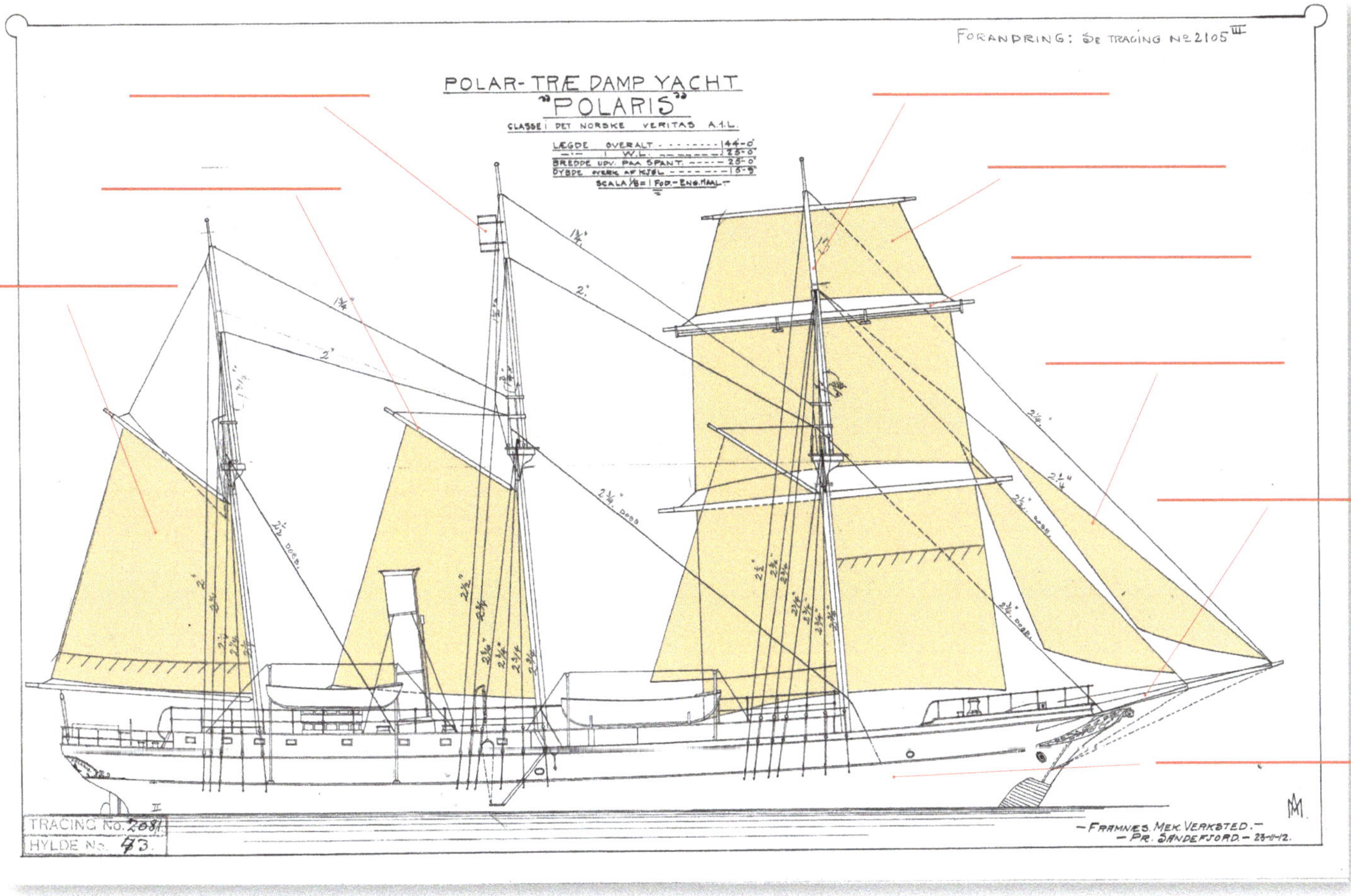

20. Shackleton's *Endurance* was a barquentine-rigged ship equipped with both sails and a steam engine. Define the term "barquentine".

____

____

21.   What is pack ice?

22.   Why do you think the *Endurance* could not run the steam engines constantly to keep breaking up the ice?

23.   What are growlers?

24.   The ship encounters massive icebergs. Where are they from?

25.   Choose two of the animals listed here (petrel, penguin, seal, or blue whale) and research how they're designed to handle the cold, harsh conditions of Antarctica.

CHAPTER 3 | THE SEA OF DECISION

Close to a month has gone by, and Leah is still hurting from Jack's departure. While working in the family supply store, the young whaler Svensen enters. Awkwardly, he tries to woo Leah and win her affection. She rejects the advances from Svensen, leading to a disagreement with her father.

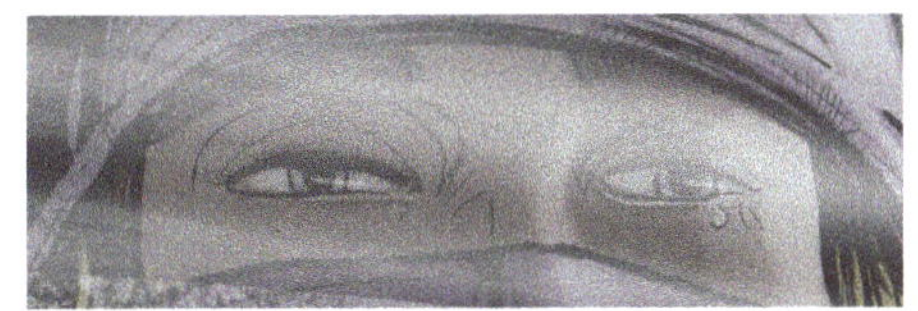

1. List all the reasons Leah responded that way to Svensen.

____

____

The *Endurance* Journey Continues

2.  Hourglass dolphins live exclusively in Antarctic waters. Research to find four other animals that are found only in Antarctica.

1. ______________________________

2. ______________________________

3. ______________________________

4. ______________________________

3. Antarctic krill, tiny shrimp-like creatures, serve as a crucial food source for many Southern Ocean animals, especially whales, and help break down carbon dioxide. Predict and describe the potential impacts on the Antarctic ecosystem if krill were to suddenly disappear.

____

____

4. Finally, the crew gets their first view of Antarctica at Coats Land. **Enter the date on page 37.**

5. How far have they traveled since entering the ice pack?

____

6. How far is the *Endurance* from Vahsel Bay? ______________ miles.

Use the scale to estimate the distance.

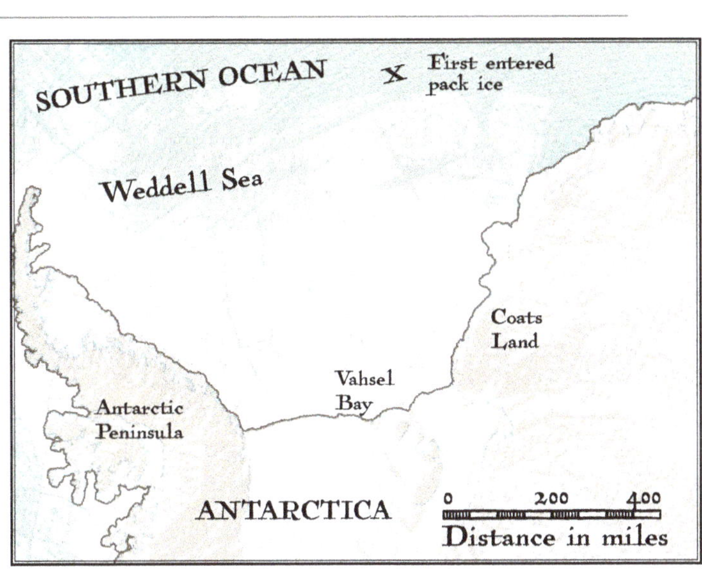

Encounter With the Ice

7. Where did Captain Worsley work before he was on the *Endurance*?

8. Compare and contrast the hazards of navigating through pack ice versus sailing through a coral reef.

9. Suddenly, the *Endurance* becomes trapped between two massive ice floes. What led to this situation?

10. Shackleton: "...*we could **heave astern** with an ice anchor and pull ourselves out in reverse...*" What does it mean to heave astern?

11. List two functions of ice anchors:

12. Despite the *Endurance* having an engine, why did the crew also require ice anchors and a capstan to free the ship from their entrapment?

Leah's Battle With the Whalers

13. Why have European whalers transitioned from the Arctic regions to the Southern Ocean?

____

____

____

14. Her strong will and activism suggest that Leah may have been influenced by the Suffragette Movement in the early 1900s. What was the Suffragette Movement?

____

____

____

15. What story does the analogy of the glass slipper come from? ______________________

16. How is Shackleton's visit from the Grim Reaper similar to Leah's visit? What happened to Leah that helped her?

____

____

17. What was the Welsh Revival of 1904-05?

____

____

____

18. What did Mrs. Cotburn say about her own life?

____

____

19. She closes with a promise for Leah: Fill in the blanks:

"God knows your battle with the _______________, He knows your _______________! You're _______________ in His eyes... He has told me He has _______________ for you... a _______________ and a _______________. Don't give up! Everything's gonna be made new again..."

The Chores and the Fight

When the boys are busy with ship chores, Perce asks Jack: "*You doin' alright? Ya haven't talked much...*"

20. As a friend, do you think Perce was: (check the best answer)

    ☐ Being too nosy, and should mind his own business?

    ☐ Really wanting to know how to help him out?

    ☐ Angry that his friend wasn't talking?

    ☐ Wanting to gossip about Jack to the crew?

In response to Perce's question, Jack answers: "*I dunno...I'm really missin' Leah... I'm worried about my brother in the war... Then here, all the mistakes I've made...and Marlow's always buggin' me!*"

21. Perce reassures him by saying:

____

____

When you or a friend are troubled about things, it's a good practice to share and even vent about the people or problems that are bothering you. We can gain insights when sharing that may help resolve the issues.

22. Packing enough food was one of the most important elements of an Antarctic expedition. Explain why it could be equally important to find fresh food, such as seal meat, along the way.

____

____

____

23. Marlow mocks Jack in front of the crew, leading to a fight between Frank Wild and Marlow. Shackleton intervenes, and Wild explains the situation to him. Why is it important for a leader to be informed about such incidents?

____

____

____

Marlow is sent to his room, and docked a week's pay. Marlow complains: "*He doesn't get it! I'm neva' gonna take the fall agin' for somethin' I didn't do...*"

24. What does Marlow say after that?

____

____

Out on the deck, Jack reflects on his experiences so far.

25. He vents to himself about Marlow's actions, then his thoughts turn to his brother, Edward, somewhere in the battlefields of Europe. World War I took place between the years 1914 and _________________

Edward and the Night on the Front Lines

26. World War I was known for trench warfare, in which armies would dig deep trenches along the front line of a battle to hide in and protect themselves. What were some of the problems that soldiers had during life in the trenches?

____

____

____

27. Do you know anyone who served in the military and had been in combat? Or a refugee from a war-torn country? Kindly ask them to share their story. You can also look online to choose a well-known veteran or refugee and learn their story. Write a short article of their experiences.

____

____

____

____

____

____

____

28. After Edward is stunned, Jack tries to wake his brother, begging Edward to tell him what he should do. Why would Jack ask for his brother's advice?

____

____

____

29. **The Destroyer soon appears.** In Revelation 9:11 in the Bible, the Destroyer is also known as who? _________________________.

30. In his dream, Edward tells Jack to find his own way. What way is he referring to?

____

____

31. The Destroyer turns and reveals himself as Marlow. How do our experiences influence our dreams when we sleep?

____

____

32. From Jack's nightmare, his spiritual struggle and fear take shape in the form of his brother on the battlefield. How does seeing his brother's death in a dream change his thinking about his own future death?

____

____

33. Find the title and author/source of each quote shown here:

1. ____________________   2. ____________________   3. ____________________

Author: ____________________   Source: ____________________   Source: ____________________

The morning breaks with a storm brewing. The crew prepares the ship to survive the storm, knowing how fierce the Antarctic weather can be. With the wind blowing hard, the combination of the wind and cold is dangerous.

34. The temperature drops to -30° F (-34.4° C). How many degrees below freezing is that temperature? You may use either the Fahrenheit or Celsius scale._____________________

Book Two, THE BECKONING SHORE
PROLOGUE

Shackleton's Dark Vision

Book Two opens with the *Endurance* expedition in dire straits: the ship is sunk, the crew's in rags, starving and dying of thirst on a small iceberg.

1.  How did Antarctic explorers in the past get fresh water to drink? How do modern-day researchers in Antarctica get fresh water?

2. How does Shackleton's nightmare foreshadow what is to come for the *Endurance*?

3. 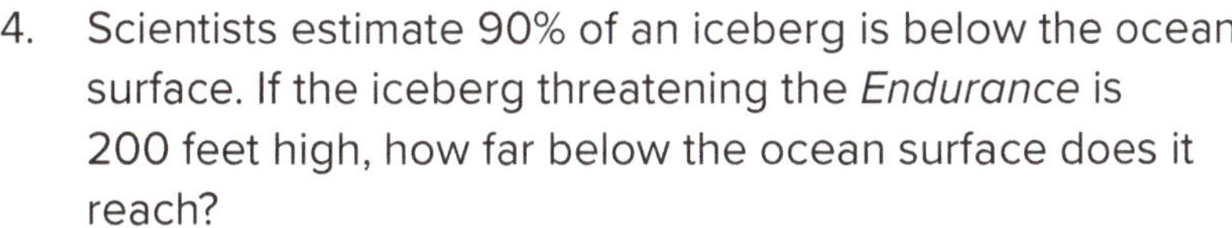 Frozen within the pack, the *Endurance* is slowly being dragged toward an immense iceberg that has run aground. What caused the berg to get stuck?

4. Scientists estimate 90% of an iceberg is below the ocean surface. If the iceberg threatening the *Endurance* is 200 feet high, how far below the ocean surface does it reach?

   500 ft.   200 ft.   1,800 ft.   900 ft.

5. The *Endurance* escapes the massive berg. What prevented the possible disaster?

The Sextant: A sextant helps seafarers navigate. It calculates latitude by measuring the angle between the horizon and the sun, moon, or a star.

6. The degree measurement is the latitude. What degree is the sextant in the diagram set to? _______________ degrees.

Longitude is calculated using two things: the GMT time zone, which sits at 0 degrees longitude, called the Prime Meridian, and the rotation of the earth, which spins at 15 degrees per hour. If you're 4 hours behind GMT (-4), multiply that time by 15 to get your longitude, which is -60 degrees.

7. You're 8 hours ahead of GMT, what would your longitude be?

____

8. What modern technology used today replaces a sextant?

____

9. Why does the U.S. Navy still require a Navigation (Deck) Officer to learn to use a sextant?

____

____

10. Label the parts of this sextant:

How Does the Sextant Work?

1. Point the sextant to the horizon.

2. Rotate the index bar on the arc to bring the sun down to the horizon. Adjust the sun's position precisely.

3. Read the angle in degrees.

The next step is to use geometry to find your position on Earth. An accurate sextant can calculate a position within one mile of your exact location.

CHAPTER 1 | THE KEEP

These three illustrations represent the polar seasons the *Endurance* is experiencing.

11. During the summer at the poles, the sun moves around the horizon in a circle and is visible nearly 24 hours a day. What causes this phenomenon?

____

____

____

12. How do sled dogs survive the frigid temperatures of Antarctica?

____

____

13. Freezing to death is called _______________________.
    Research and write below what happens to the
    body when this occurs.

____

____

14. A person can survive in a blizzard if they bury themselves under the snow. Why is
    that true?

____

____

Edward's Battle in France

15. When did the Battle of Loos, France take place?

    _______________________________. **Add this to page 37.**

16. Some wars are labeled as justified, others are not.
    What do you think the phrase, "A Just War" means?

____

____

____

17. Write a paragraph about the Battle of Loos, a significant event in World War I.
    Include details such as the year it occurred, the number of British soldiers wounded
    and killed, and the outcome of the battle.

____

____

____

____

The Endurance Hull Cracks

18. Months have passed since the ship has been locked in its icy prison. The pressure from the unrelenting pack ice is taking its toll. The ship creaked and moaned, and finally, on October ________, ______________, the ice won. A wave of pressure lifted her, twisted the ship, and broke the keel and rudder. **Add this date to page 37**.

19. What factors contribute to the pressure within pack ice?

20. What is the keel of a ship?

Shackleton gathers his men on the ice to explain their predicament.

21. A good leader will assess the situation as honestly as possible. What were some of the things the Boss said to help the despondent crew?

22. Explain why a blubber stove was beneficial to bring on an Antarctic expedition.

23. What are Shackleton's top concerns and what he hopes for concerning their predicament?

CHAPTER 2 | THE FROZEN SEA

Ernest Shackleton had this observation: *"...Huge blocks of ice, weighing many tons, were lifted into the air and tossed aside as other masses rose beneath them. We were helpless intruders in a strange world, our lives dependent upon the play of grim elementary forces that made a mock of our puny efforts."*

1. What is causing the "grim elementary forces" Shackleton describes? How does his observation about the ice blocks reflect the challenges faced by his expedition in Antarctica?

____

____

____

____

2. The *Endurance*, sank on _______________________, 1915. **Enter this date on page 37.**

3. The ice beneath Ocean Camp begins to shift and put the crew in danger. Shackleton decides to make for Paulet Island. When did they begin their march on the ice? _______________. **Enter on page 37.**

4. Fill in the blanks on the map, based on the text from page 37 in *The Beckoning Shore* and the timeline map on p.6-7.

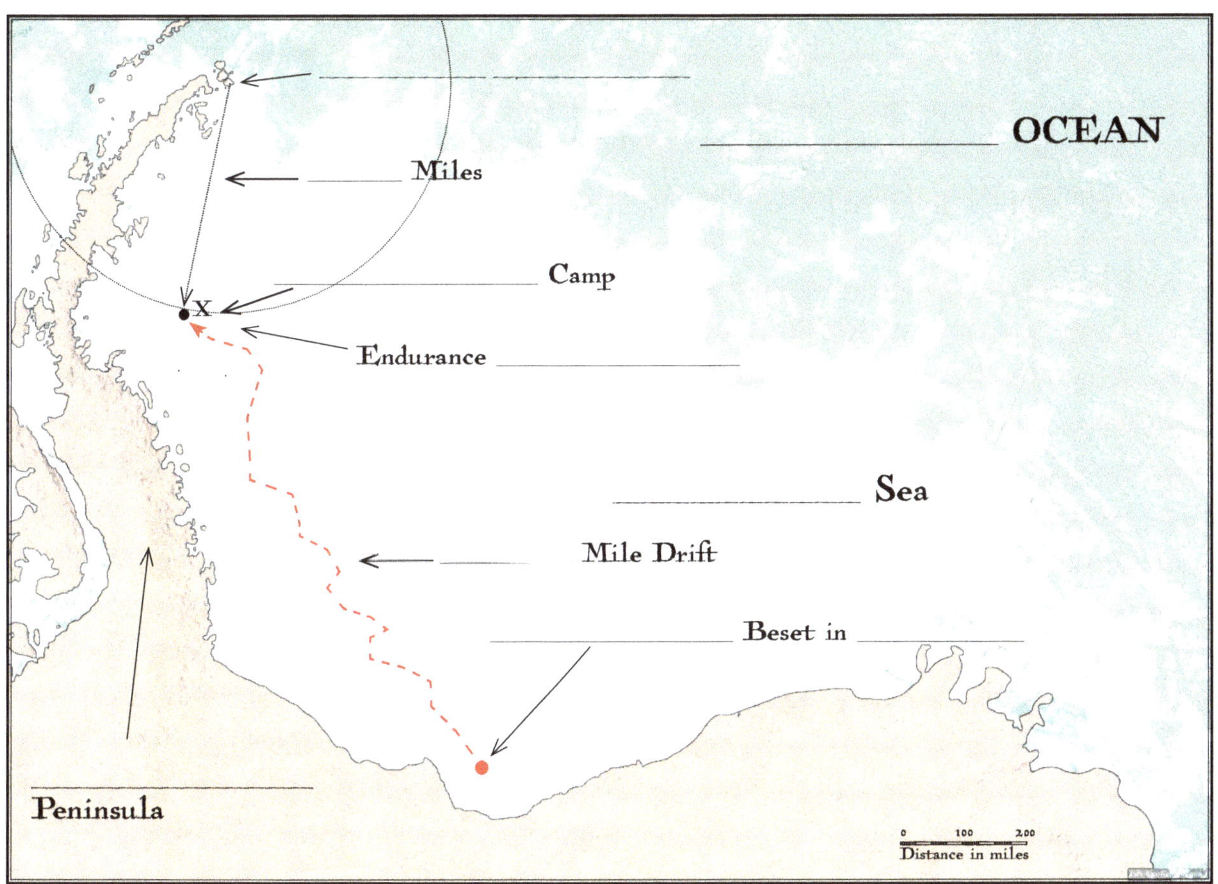

The men have to pull the sleds themselves and they soon find out how difficult it is. Shackleton writes:

"...The first 200 yards took us about five hours to cross, owing to the amount of breaking down of pressure-ridges and filling in of leads that was required. The surface, too, was now very soft, so our progress was slow and tiring..."

Shackleton overseeing the pulling of the boats December 1915.

Photograph by Frank Hurley.
Image courtesy of Royal Geographical Society

5. What is a pressure ridge? What can cause their formation?

6. Shackleton refers to a *lead...* What is that?

7. Why was the surface very soft?

8. In Antarctica in the month of November, what season is it? Check the correct answer.

    Winter   Spring   Summer   Autumn

The Mutiny

9. Why do you think some of the crew would disagree with Shackleton's decision to pack up the boats and head to Paulet Island?

10. When Shackleton confronts McNeish, he has Wild and Worsley carrying firearms at his back. Why?

11. McNeish's argument calls for them to dump the boats and by using the dogs, march to the island faster. Why did Shackleton's plan to escape include the boats?

12. McNeish says that the Boss is no longer in charge. What was Shackleton's response?

13. If you were in this situation, who would you follow? Shackleton and his slow, methodical path, or McNeish and his quick path? Explain your answer.

The March Ends

14. On the 29th of December, the march with the boats ended. What was the reason for this?

15. Add an entry to the timeline on page 37. What season is it now? ___________________

16. Why did the crew call their new base Patience Camp?

Endurance to Buenos Aires from Plymouth
Island of South Georgia
Island of South Georgia
Stromness
King Haakon Bay
Grytviken
Buenos Aires
Elephant Island
Punta Arenas
Weddell Sea
Coats Land
Southern Ocean
ANTARCTICA
South Pole
Amundsen reaches South Pole
Scott and his men perish
McMurdo Sound
Ross Sea
Sandefjord
NORWAY
ENGLAND
London
Plymouth
GERMANY
Loos
FRANCE

Timeline and Map of *Endurance: The Frozen Keep & The Beckoning Shore*

Chronicling Ernest Shackleton's Imperial Trans-Antarctic Expedition and The Great War.

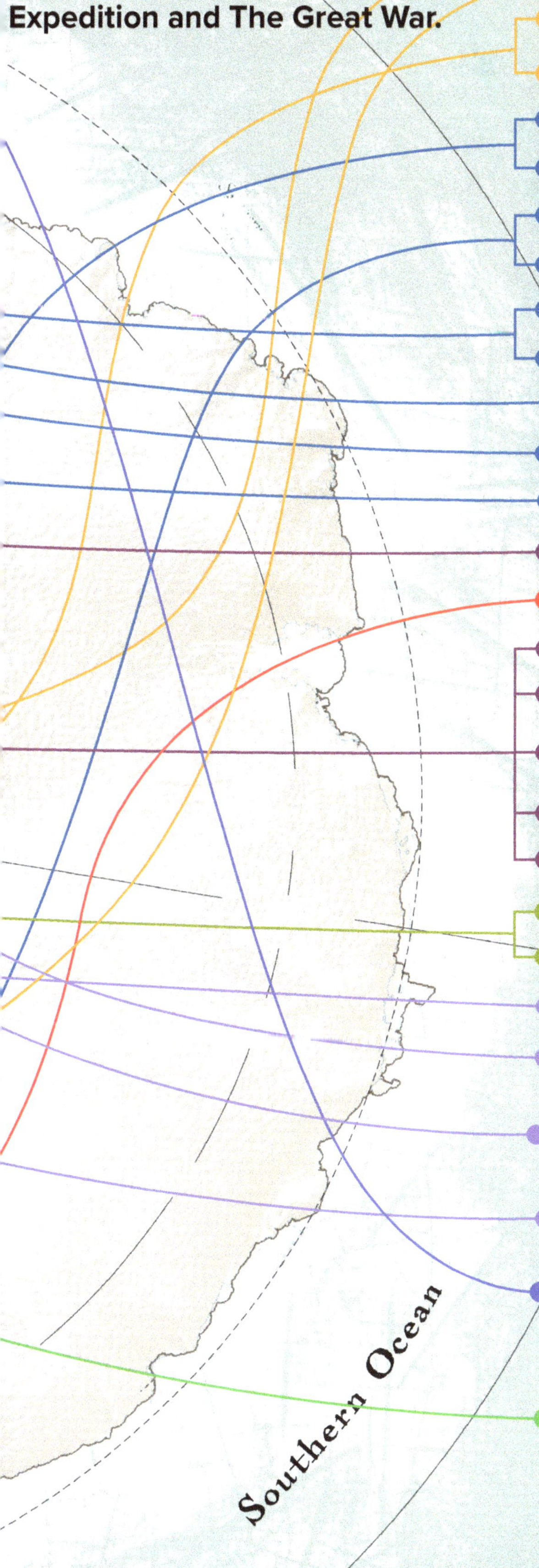

Timeline of Events 1904 - 2022

Month/Day/Year	Event	
	Grytviken, South Georgia established as Southern Ocean whaling station.	P.13
	Norway's Amundsen reaches South Pole.	P.19
	UK's Scott and party perish on ice.	P.19
	Polaris built in Sandefjord, Norway.	P.21
	Shackleton purchases *Endurance*.	P.21
August 1, 1914	*Endurance* departs London.	
August 1, 1914	Germany declares war on Russia	
	England declares war on Germany	P.15
August 8, 1914	*Endurance* departs Plymouth	
October 26, 1914	*Endurance* leaves Buenos Aires.	
November 5, 1914	*Endurance* arrives at Grytviken.	
	The Expedition departs Grytviken.	P.17
	Endurance enters the Antarctic pack ice.	P.21
	First sighting of Antarctica at Coats Land.	P.23
January 18, 1915	*Endurance* becomes beset in the pack ice.	
	Battle of Loos, France.	P.31
	Endurance wrecks. Crew abandons ship.	P.32
	Ocean Camp built.	P.35
	Endurance sinks to the bottom of the Weddell Sea—not to be seen until 2022.	P.33
	Crew begins march.	P.33
	March halted, Patience Camp set up.	P.35
	Lifeboats launched.	P.42
	The men land on Elephant Island.	P.47
	James Caird sails for South Georgia.	P.50
	James Caird arrives at King Haakon Bay, South Georgia.	P.51
	Shackleton, Worsley, and Crean cross mountains, arrive at Stromness.	P.54
	Expedition survivors rescued from Elephant Island.	P.57
	Shackleton dies at age 46 in Grytviken, South Georgia.	P.58
	Signing of the Antarctic Treaty.	P.11
	*Endurance*22 discovers the *Endurance* resting on the bottom of the Weddell Sea.	P.59

17. Being so long on the ice, the food supply is running low. What does the Boss decide about the dogs?

Orde-Lees Encounters a Leopard Seal

18. Leopard seals are one of the apex predators in Antarctica. The other is the orca. What is an apex predator?

19. Describe the characteristics and behavior of leopard seals using multiple sources.

20. **The first recorded attack on a human is from our story.** A large leopard seal attacked Thomas Orde-Lees when Shackleton's expedition was at Patience Camp in 1916. Research and find 3 other reported attacks by leopard seals. Write a short paragraph describing what happened in each instance.

A Blizzard Hits Patience Camp

21. The men have to huddle around the camp stove for warmth. Since there were no trees nor wood on the frozen sea, what fuel was used to heat the stove?

22. Even in dire moments, some good comes from misfortune. What does Worsley say about the storm?

23. Why does being pushed north help their plight?

24. After the storm was over, what did the crew discover about the dogs?

Shackleton gathered his men and said: "*Due to the food shortages and the long reach of the sea, and how far we are from land, the use of the dogs for hauling supplies has come to an end...We've decided to put down all the animals for mercy's sake. We will not leave them on the ice to suffer a cruel death! To help us avoid starvation, the young dogs will be taken for food for us...They served us well and many of us will miss their companionship...I am sorry...*"

25. Shackleton says *It's for the best.* That was no consolation for the men…the companionship of the dogs was a bright light in a cold, dark world…What is the saying about dogs and men? *A dog is man's* _______________ _______________.

The Wreckage Found

26. A whaling ship encounters the debris floating in the water and identifies it as remnants from the *Endurance* shipwreck. Discuss two modern techniques used in rescue operations to locate shipwrecks.

27. What is the Bible verse in the quote: *"All Your breakers and Your waves have rolled over me"*

28. In retrospect, Shackleton was criticized for not purchasing certain equipment for the expedition, which could have sent out a distress call to be heard by rescuers. What was this equipment and what was its capabilities? What were his reasons, if any, for not acquiring it?

29. Paul the apostle's fantastic voyage from the Bible gives a first-hand account of a small wooden ship in a heavy storm. Read Acts chapter 27 and compare Paul's experience with that of the *Endurance*.

CHAPTER 3 | STRANGERS IN A STRANGE LAND

1. Nearing starvation, Shackleton and Worsley plot the next move for the crew. They see Joinville Island on the horizon, but Shackleton decides against going there, opting instead for Elephant Island. On the  map, find and label Joinville Island and Elephant Island.

2. Worsley calculates Elephant Island is 100 miles due north of their present location. Place a small X on the map where you think the marooned men are located. Which island is closer? _______________________________. *(Each circle is 50 miles.)*

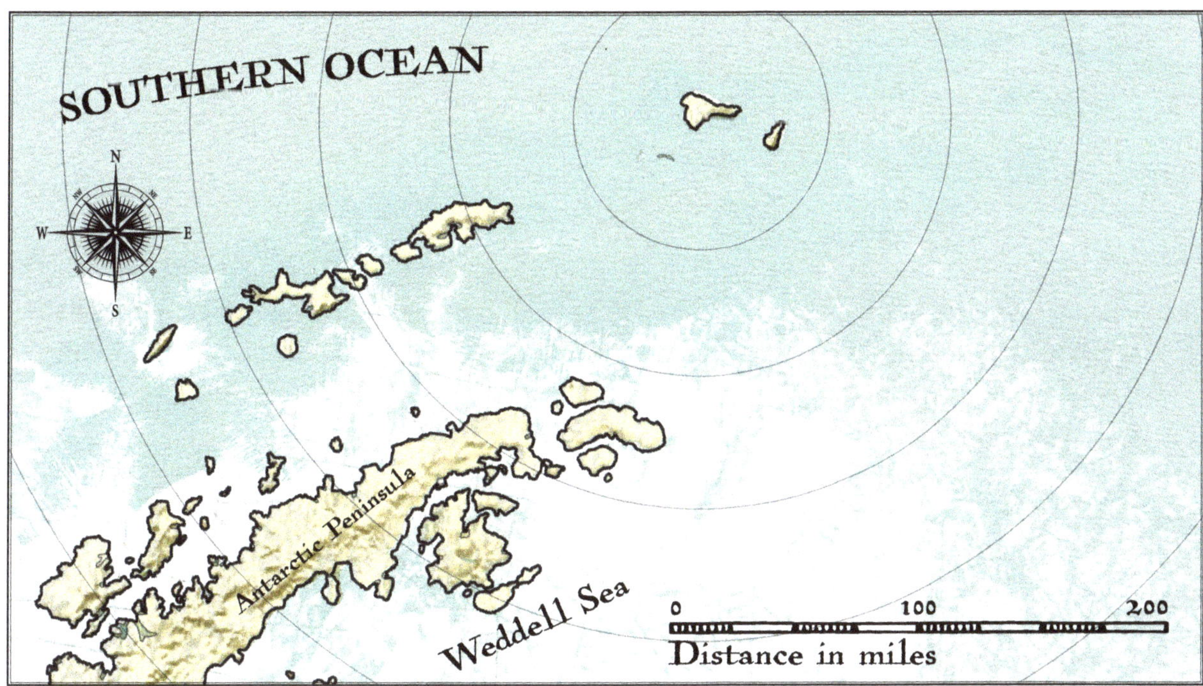

3. Why did the Boss not want to try for Joinville Island?

____

____

4. The northward drift of the pack ice in the Weddell Sea is caused by the **Weddell Gyre**. Describe what that is and the factors contributing to its existence.

____

____

____

____

Shackleton writes days later on April 8, 1916: *"...The pack is much looser this morning, and the long, rolling swell from the northeast is more pronounced than it was yesterday. The floes rise and fall with the surge of the sea. We evidently are drifting with the surface current, for all the heavier masses of floe and bergs are being left behind..."*

5. What is the scientific cause for the "long rolling swell" observed by the crew?

6. What factors contribute to ice floes breaking apart?

7. Finally, next day, April 9, 1916... *"The call to action came at 1 p.m. The pack opened well and the channels became navigable...it is best not to wait any longer...* **Add the boats' launch day to the timeline on page 37**

8. After hearing the crew give luck and good fortune all the credit for their survival, what does Shackleton finally tell the crew about what has truly guided them?

9. The three little boats are in the middle of the sea with a giant swell and icebergs crashing all around. How does Shackleton feel in that moment after their narrow escape?

10. With the weather finally clearing, the tiny boats enter a glorious scene...What specific species of Antarctic animals might the crew have observed?

11. Many Antarctic birds are pelagic. What does "pelagic" mean, and why might a pelagic bird be found near land?

12. Research and make a list of 5 facts about Adélie penguins that distinguish them from other penguins.

    1. _______________________________
    2. _______________________________
    3. _______________________________
    4. _______________________________
    5. _______________________________

Andrew Shiva / Wikipedia / CC BY-SA 4.0

13. Both historical boats and modern boats often have their bottoms painted white. Research to find out what kind of paint it is, and why it's used.

Orca or killer whale (Orcinus orca)

14. What does Orcinus orca translate to in English?

15. What is the orca most closely related to, a whale or a dolphin? _______________________________

16. In what oceans and seas are orcas found?

17. What are some of the characteristics that make the orca unique?

18. What is the average life span of an orca?_______________________________

19. What is the average size and weight of an orca? _______________________________ .

    Use a tape measure and mark off the average size and see how big they can grow to be!

20. Research a recent news story about orcas, and then write a short paragraph detailing the event.

____

____

____

____

____

The Cracked Floe

The crew finds a suitable floe to camp that night after the long day of paddling with the oars. After everyone eats and sets up tents, Jack takes first watch so the others can sleep. Shackleton, disturbed by an uneasy feeling, joins him at his watch. Suddenly, the floe cracks in two, and with shouts, a tent plunges into the void.

21. After rescuing the men, they see the *James Caird* sitting on the split floe and is starting to drift away. If they had lost the lifeboat and had only two lifeboats left for the 29 men, why would that be dangerous for the crew? Explain your reasoning.

____

____

____

22. After taking a navigational reading to calculate their distance to Elephant Island, Shackleton discovered they had drifted backwards 30 miles. They decided not to reveal this to the crew. What factors in the Weddell Sea might have caused them to drift backwards?

____

____

____

____

23. Before launching the boats the crew discarded more supplies, some of them much needed. Why did they do that?

24. Shackleton and his men now need to sail west to reach Elephant Island. On the map, mark the approximate location of the boats based on their new heading. Explain the factors that led to their drift eastward, such as the influence of ocean currents, ice movement, and prevailing winds.

25. **Leah plans her future.** *The Times of London* was one of the world's most widely read newspapers in the early 1900s. What is Leah's letter to *The Times* about, what does she hope will happen to the letter, and what kind of impact does Leah think the letter will have?

26. Leah notices a painting crew working, an idea pops in her mind, and she decides to go forward with it. Based on her self-talk, what is her justification for what she is about to do?

27. The next morning, Joe discovers someone had painted graffiti over the new paint, *Stop the Slaughter!* The factory boss immediately knew who did it...He marches to the Carlberg residence and confronts Leah's parents on the misdeed. Her father goes directly into Leah's room, finds the evidence, and confronts her. With the evidence, Leah is caught and can't lie or deny she did the misdeed. What was her reaction?

28. Leah acted out alone in anger and desperation.
    Did it help or hurt her cause? Explain your answer.

29. There have been protests against whaling which
    created international news headlines. List some
    organizations and their past protests that have
    helped bring a sustained pause to whaling.

Braving the Sea

30. The three small boats are sailing the treacherous Southern Ocean, hoping to make
    landfall. *"...Sleeting gales that freeze their beards and coat the boats heavily with ice..."*
    Define what a sleeting gale is.

31. They run out of fresh water and while eating raw seal meat,
    they swallow the blood to overcome thirst. Why didn't
    that help?

32. Why did Shackleton and his crew avoid drinking ocean water? Explain the effects
    of drinking seawater to quench thirst.

33. They encounter ice floating near them. Research sea ice to answer these questions: How much salt is in sea ice when it is formed, and is it safe to drink?

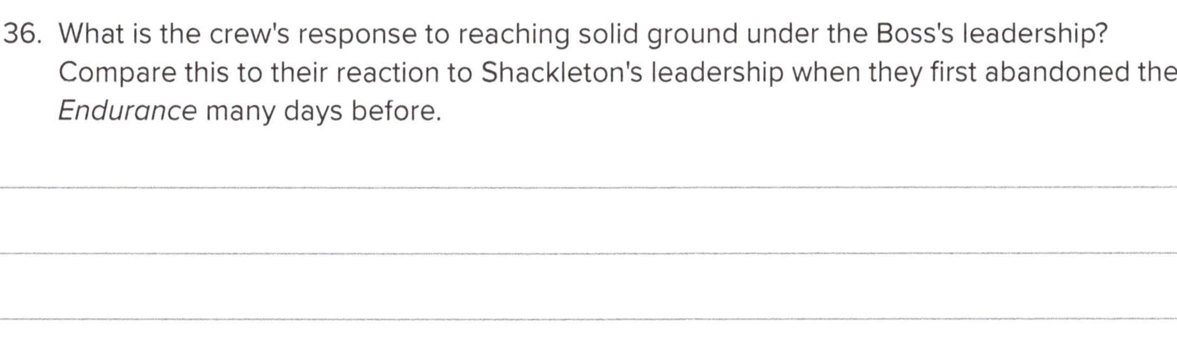

At one point Shackleton despaired: *"...Rest was not for us...The temperature was below zero and the wind penetrated our clothes and chilled us almost unbearably. I doubted if all the men would survive that night..."* And just when it seems all hope is lost: *"...With the dawn the weather cleared...A magnificent sunrise heralded in what we hoped would be our last day in the boats..."* Suddenly, Shackleton cries out: *"There she is boys! Elephant Island!"*

34. Finding no landing, the boats rounded the headland to the north side. What is a headland?

35. On 16 April, 1916, after seven grueling days at sea, the lifeboats land safely on Elephant Island. **Add this date to page 37.** From that morning so long ago when the *Endurance* sailed from Grytviken, until this point in time, calculate the number of days since the crew had set foot on land. Use the timeline on page 37 for reference.

_______________________ days.

36. What is the crew's response to reaching solid ground under the Boss's leadership? Compare this to their reaction to Shackleton's leadership when they first abandoned the *Endurance* many days before.

37. On the map, draw a dotted line representing the approach the crew took to Elephant Island. Remember, they were southeast of the island and the wind blows from west to east.

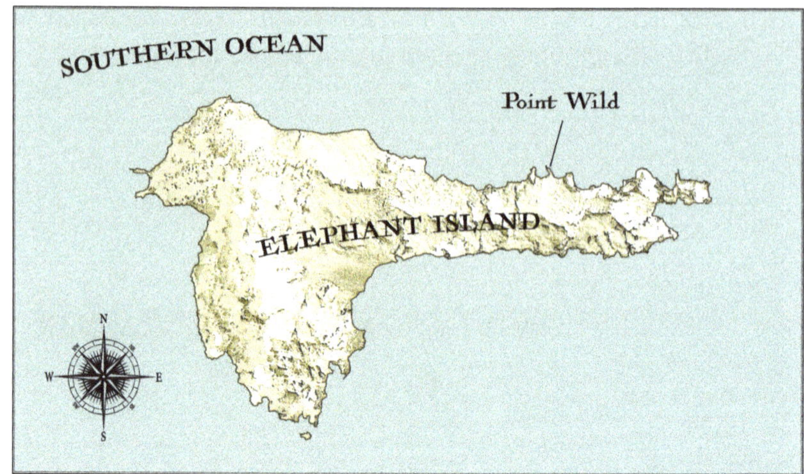

CHAPTER 4 | THE BECKONING SHORE

Edward is Awaiting Another Battle...

1. In the trenches on a long forgotten battlefield, the British infantry is preparing for an enemy attack. Edward has now been on the frontlines for over a year. What has changed about Edward?

2. What is infantry?

3. The Battle of Loos was waged in the fall of 1915. Since then, the horrors of war necessitated a much needed upgrade in equipment. What is one major change that took place in the uniforms? Explain why.

4. What is artillery?

5. The Germans fire on the British artillery units far behind Edward. Why there?

After the onslaught, the British artillerymen man their cannons and respond in kind.

6. Mortars are fired from the German lines. What are mortars? Why was it feared by infantry in the trenches?

____

____

7. On the battlefield, what was the average distance between trenches of the combatants in World War I? _______________________________________

8. What was the strip of land between enemy trenches called?

____

The trenches are overwhelmed by the Germans, Edward is shot, and falls onto the muddy ground....*And I declared that the dead, who had already died, are happier than the living, who are still alive, But better than both is the one who has never been born, who has not seen the evil that is done under the sun...* (Ecclesiastes 4:3 4, NIV)

9. This quoted Bible text from King Solomon is an example of hyperbole. What is hyperbole, and how does Solomon's hyperbole relate to the horrors of war?

____

____

____

____

10. Can you name some of the wars and conflicts you have heard of or seen in your life?

____

____

The Desperate Gamble

11. On Elephant Island, the realization of the predicament the expedition crew is in begins to dawn on Shackleton. What are his concerns?

____

____

12. Shackleton, with his expedition leaders, craft a desperate gamble. The next morning, the Boss shares the details with the crew. Describe the plan.

13. Why must they make the trip to South Georgia before winter hits?

14. Although it is not covered in our story, research how Frank Wild and the marooned crew survived while they waited on Elephant Island.

The *James Caird* was modified by raising the sides at least 10 inches, and by adding a deck with canvas on top to keep out the water for their voyage. Once finished, the small group said goodbye to their fellow crew members.

15. The *James Caird* was launched on April _______, 1916. **Enter on page 37.**

16. Chart the course by drawing a line from where they are on Elephant Island to the Island of South Georgia It is approximately __________ miles.

The Storm

As the tiny boat encounters a storm, Shackleton begins to sing a sea shanty.

17. "Fish in the Sea" is a traditional shanty originally sung by Scottish fishermen. Research sea shanties to find out what their purpose was.

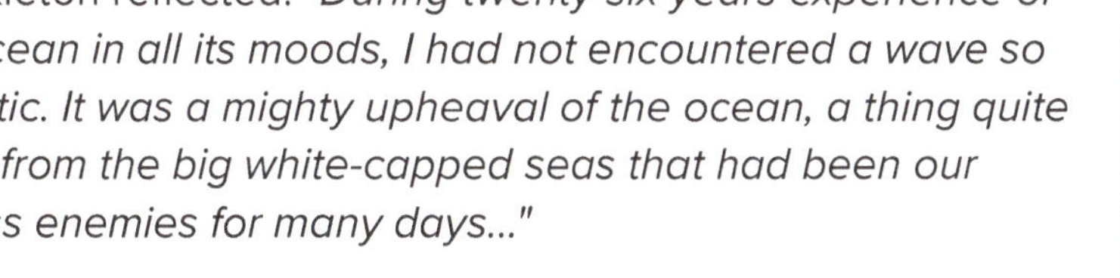

____

____

____

18. Write your own sea shanty, and include things that you might see and experience while on a ship at sea. Also include things or people you might miss on land. It can be serious or humorous.

____

____

____

____

19. Suddenly he notices a change on the horizon. What did he think it was?

____

The Rogue Wave

20. Fear overwhelms the men, but the Boss thinks fast. What does he believe they need to have to survive this wave?

____

Shackleton reflected: "_During twenty-six years experience of the ocean in all its moods, I had not encountered a wave so gigantic. It was a mighty upheaval of the ocean, a thing quite apart from the big white-capped seas that had been our tireless enemies for many days..._"

Finally, "Land Ho!"

21. Anxious to make landfall, what do they discover as they get close to the island?

____

____

22. How long did they have to wait offshore to finally land the _James Caird_? _______________
    Add the date they arrived onshore to page 37.

23. Jack becomes very sick and is in need of medicine and care. What does the Boss determine to do?

24. What potential dangers might Shackleton and his companions encounter during their trek through the mountains of South Georgia Island?

Leah

25. After reading the letter from *The Times of London*, Leah is in a complex situation... What are some reasons her going to England would be hurtful to her parents?

26. Shackleton, Worsley and Crean are slowly making their way up the mountains from sea level. It is very difficult in their weakened condition, with their poor clothing and primitive equipment. Research and identify two items used today for mountain climbing and hiking in snow and ice. For each item, explain its function.

At King Haakon Bay, Marlow Comes Clean

As it turns evening, Jack asks Marlow a very vulnerable question: *"Why do ya hate me so much?"* Marlow answers with a devastating story of what had happened to him in his past: *"...I was aboard a clipper headin' for Hong Kong, when a gale started blowin'...The foreman ordered us aloft to reef the sails."*

27. Match the words to their meaning by drawing a line connecting them:

    clipper   supervises and directs other workers

    gale   taking in or rolling up a sail to reduce the area exposed to the wind

    foreman   Large merchant sailing ship that plied global routes and ferried cargo and passengers

    aloft   a strong wind

    reef   at, on, or to the masthead or the higher rigging

28. If you were an investigator, describe what happened aloft on that fateful evening based on the testimonies.

    ____

    ____

    ____

    ____

29. How are clipper ships and junk ships different from each other? How are freighter ships different from clippers and junks?

    ____

    ____

    ____

30. What was the purpose of the Suez Canal, and when and where was it constructed?

    ____

    ____

    ____

    ____

31. Following the text, draw a line on the map of Marlow's journey back to England through the Suez Canal. For comparison, chart a course from Hong Kong to England traveling around Africa.

32. **Back in the mountains,** the men finally spot the whaling town of Stromness. What date did they walk into Stromness?

____

Enter on page 37.

This is a hand-drawn map by Shackleton, created from memory, to illustrate the route they took across South Georgia. This was included in his journal, *South*, the complete story of this epic journey from the Boss himself.

33. Estimate how many miles or kilometers it is from King Haakon Bay to Stromness in a straight line, using the scale provided.

It is________ miles/km.

34. Go online and compare a satellite image of South Georgia with Shackleton's map. The difference is notable! For fun, draw a map of your neighborhood from memory, then look at an actual map of your neighborhood from the internet and compare.

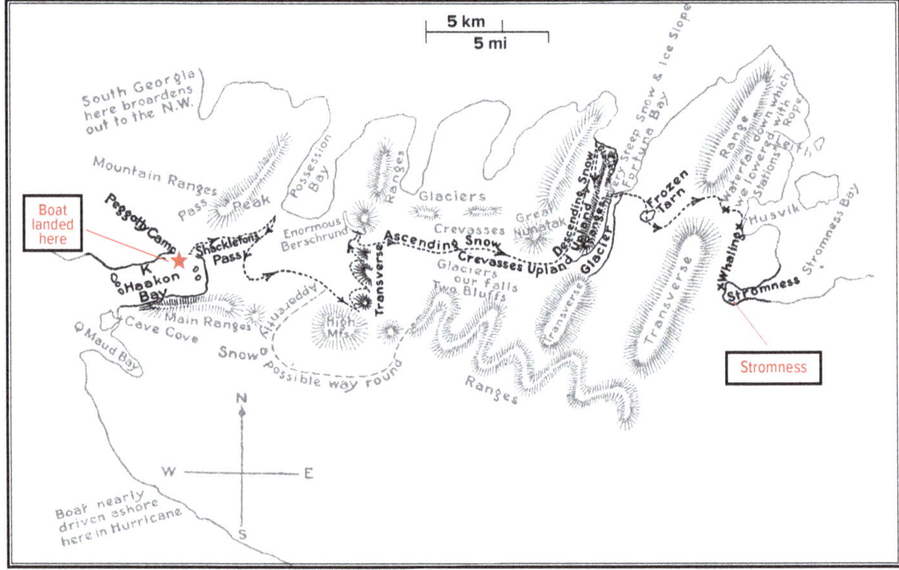

35. Shackleton said in looking back on the crossing: *"...I have no doubt that Providence guided us...that we were four, not three..."* *Providence* is a word little used today. What do you think he meant using that word?

Leah Departs the Island

36. Leah's leaving for Norway. She has changed her plans unbeknownst to her parents. What is Leah determined to do?

Mrs. Cotburn and the Supervisor

37. A message arrives through a telegraph machine. Explain what a telegraph machine is, including its history and purpose.

38. Describe the Morse Code language's function and attributes. Is it still in use today? Explain.

39. Please translate this word using the translator at right:

· —· —·· ·— ·—· ·— —· —·— ·

40. Using a flashlight or something you can tap, send a one-word Morse Code message to a friend or family member. Try it once with the recipient in the same room with you, then try it again with the recipient in a different room.

41. How does Leah's reaction to the news about Jack, which disrupts her plans to go to England, reflect her priorities and decision-making process? Why did she choose to return to Grytviken instead?

____

____

____

International Morse Code

1. The length of a dot is one unit.
2. A dash is three units.
3. The space between parts of the same letter is one unit.
4. The space between letters is three units.
5. The space between words is seven units.

A	·—		U	··—
B	—···		V	···—
C	—·—·		W	·——
D	—··		X	—··—
E	·		Y	—·——
F	··—·		Z	——··
G	——·			
H	····			
I	··			
J	·———		1	·————
K	—·—		2	··———
L	·—··		3	···——
M	——		4	····—
N	—·		5	·····
O	———		6	—····
P	·——·		7	——···
Q	——·—		8	———··
R	·—·		9	————·
S	···		0	—————
T	—			

42. Back in King Haakon Bay, if Shackleton, Worsley and Crean had not made it in their march over the mountains of South Georgia, list 3 actions Jack and Marlow could have done to possibly be rescued.

____

____

____

____

____

The Rescue from Elephant Island

43. Three months later, Shackleton is on his final rescue attempt of Frank Wild and the *Endurance* crew, still marooned on Elephant Island. The *Yelcho* is described as a tugboat. What is the proper use of this sort of boat?

____

____

____

____

44.  What does *"Capitan! Tierra a la vista!"* translate into English? Use an online translator to figure out the language and the translation.

45. What was the date Shackleton rescued the survivors? _________________. **Enter date on page 37.**

46. As a leader, his main concern was his men's welfare. What are the first words Shackleton shouts to the crew? _______________________________

The Not So Glorious Return

47. The *Yelcho* had a triumphal return to Chile after her successful mission to rescue the men of the *Endurance*. How were the men of the expedition received in England upon their return, and what factors influenced the public's response? When did Shackleton return?

____

____

____

____

____

The Characters of *Endurance*, the Graphic Novel Series

48. While some of the characters, such as Jack Robinson and Leah Carlberg, aren't real people, why are their fictional roles valuable to a nonfiction story?

____

____

____

____

Answer the questions below from the bios on page 137. You may have to research online to find some of the answers.

Sir Ernest Shackleton | 1874 —1922

49. Shackleton took part in how many Antarctic expeditions?

____

50. The date of his death? **Enter on page 37.**

51. Where is he buried? _______________________________

52. At the time of his death, he was deeply in _______________.

Frank Wild | 1873 —1939

53. Wild joined _______ expeditions to Antarctica.

54. He was awarded the _______________________ with four bars, one of only two men to be so honored.

55. Wild died in 1939, but when and where was he finally buried?

____

Frank Worsley | 1872 —1943

56. He was _______________ of the *Endurance*.

57. Worsley's expert _______________________ skills were responsible for the survival of the entire expedition party.

58. In 1922, he sailed with _______________ on his final Antarctic expedition.

Tom Crean | 1877 — 1938

59. During Scott's 1913 Terra Nova Expedition where Scott and his party _______________, Crean hiked _____________ miles alone across the ice to try save the life of Edward Evans.

60. How many Antarctic expeditions did Crean go on? _______

Perce Blackborow | 1896—1949

61. Perce came on board the *Endurance* as a _____________.

62. He suffered _______________________ on Elephant Island and lost his _______________________ to amputation.

63. He received the Bronze _______________ Medal for his service.

EPILOGUE

64. **Fast forward to 2022...**What was the name of the expedition to finally find the lost ship *Endurance*?

65. There were engineers, geophysicists, medical scientists, oceanographers, computer scientists, explorers, mechanical engineers, among others, that were part of the crew. Why were so many types of occupations needed for this expedition?

The stern of the *Endurance*.
© Falklands Maritime Heritage Trust

66. How deep below the surface was the *Endurance* finally found? _______________

67. **Protected as a historical site under the Antarctic Treaty, it will stay where it was found...**What does it mean to "be protected as a historical site"?

Retrieving the SAAB Sabertooth underwater vehicle after a test dive.

68. The *Endurance* was discovered on _______________ ,2022. **Add this date on page 37.**

The Endurance Series Workbook Answer Key

This Answer Key is an assorted list of solutions to the problems and exercises in this workbook, with the idea of the best possible answers written in. They may not be the only correct answer for the student, as the statement, "Answers may vary" appears where appropriate.

Fill-in answers for map on page 36-37

TIMELINE OF EVENTS 1904 - 2022

MONTH/DAY/YEAR	EVENT
November 16, 1904	Grytviken, South Georgia established as Southern Ocean whaling station
December 14, 1911	Amundsen reaches South Pole
March 29, 1912	UK's Scott and party perish on ice
December 17, 1912	*Polaris* built in Sandefjord, Norway
January 1914	Shackleton purchases *Endurance*
August 1, 1914	*Endurance* departs London
August 1, 1914	Germany declares war on Russia
August 4, 1914	England declares war on Germany
August 8, 1914	*Endurance* departs Plymouth
October 26, 1914	*Endurance* leaves Buenos Aires
November 5, 1914	*Endurance* arrives at Grytviken
December 5, 1914	The Expedition departs Grytviken
December 7, 1914	*Endurance* enters the Antarctic pack ice
January 10, 1915	First sighting of Antarctica at Coats Land
January 18, 1915	*Endurance* becomes beset in the pack ice
Sept 25-Oct. 8, 1915	Battle of Loos, France
October 27, 1915	The crew abandons the *Endurance*
November 1, 1915	Ocean Camp built
November 21, 1915	*Endurance* sinks to the bottom of the Weddell Sea—not to be seen until 2022
December 23, 1915	Crew begins march
December 29, 1915	March halted. Patience Camp set up
April 9, 1916	Lifeboats launched
April 16, 1916	The men land on Elephant Island
April 24, 1916	*James Caird* sails for South Georgia
May 10, 1916	*James Caird* arrives at King Haakon Bay, South Georgia
May 20, 1916	Shackleton, Worsley, and Crean cross mountains, arrive at Stromness
August 30, 1916	Expedition survivors rescued from Elephant Island
January 5, 1922	Shackleton dies at age 46 in Grytviken, South Georgia
December 1, 1959	Signing of the Antarctic Treaty
March 5, 2022	*Endurance*22 discovers the *Endurance* deep beneath the surface of the Weddell Sea

Book One, The Frozen Keep

1. **Keep** (*kēp*): (v) to restrain from departure or removal; (n) the strongest and securest part of a medieval castle; a prison.

2. It's both a place of security and imprisonment

Introduction / Prologue

3. The primary objective of the *Endurance* expedition, which began in August 1914, was to be the first to cross the vast, uncharted continent of Antarctica. This ambitious goal aimed to expand the boundaries of human exploration and scientific knowledge.

4. The departure of the *Endurance* occurred just as Great Britain declared war on Germany, marking the beginning of World War I. As the nation became consumed with the conflict, the expedition and its brave crew received little attention, making their journey a largely overlooked yet significant chapter in the annals of exploration.

5. She smelled the foul odor of whale carcasses.

6. Answers may vary. She regrets her family's decision to come to Grytviken.

7. Leah was determined to leave as soon as possible, never to return.

8. A hand-thrown harpoon relies on the physical strength and skill of the whaler to accurately strike the whale, which limits the range and force of the projectile. The cannon harpoon can propel a harpoon farther, faster, and more accurately, which would greatly increase the number of whales caught.

9. Charting or navigating.

10. In 1914, airplanes were a fairly new invention, and ships were still the standard mode of long-distance transportation. The first flight over Antarctica was in 1929, and the first plane to land in Antarctica was in 1956.

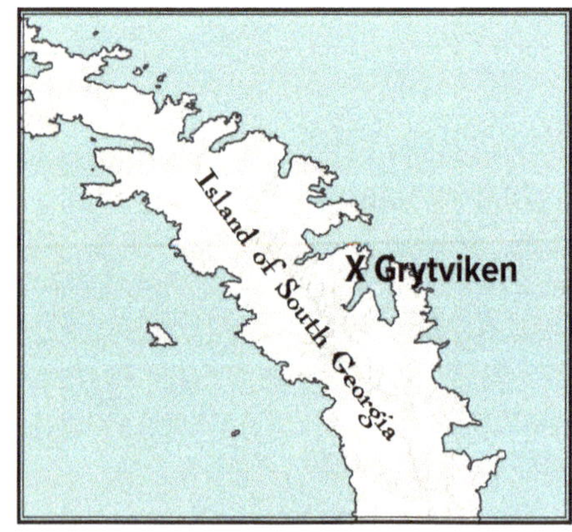

11. See map

Chapter 1 | A Far Country

12. They were amazed at the size of the whale bones. They also observed the smell of death and decay. Their talked turned to the war in Europe that became known as World War I.

13. Whale oil could be used to create nitroglycerin, a key component in ammunition. The oil also worked well as a machine lubricant, and many machines were built and used during the war.

14. Jack's brother Edward quit the expedition to join the British Army at the start of the war.

15. Radio equipment, lights, generator, wiring, batteries, connections.

16. The Germans are boasting how Germany will win the war.

17. Leah is frustrated because her plans to leave are moving too slow. She has little money saved.

18. They want to annoy the Brits: Jack, Perce and Frank Wild.

19. He is accusing Frank Wild of cowardice.

20. Foreshadowing is a literary device used by authors to give hints or clues about events that will occur later in the story. The *Endurance*—and Frank Wild—will soon be shipwrecked.

21. Answers may vary. They're braving harsh weather, the possibility of starvation and death, the unknown, etc.

22. Answers will vary. **The Hope Bay incident** occurred in 1952 between Argentina and the United Kingdom. This conflict arose over territorial claims in Antarctica, with both nations establishing research stations at Hope Bay. The Argentine forces fired warning shots when a British team attempted to build a hut nearby, escalating tensions over the disputed territory.
The Deception Island incident, part of the larger context of the Antarctic territorial disputes, took place in 1958. The United Kingdom and Chile clashed when British forces dismantled a Chilean hut on Deception Island, further straining relations over sovereignty claims in Antarctica.
The Falklands War occurred in 1982 between Argentina and the United Kingdom, with Argentina invading the Falkland Islands, which were under British control. The conflict was rooted in long-standing sovereignty disputes over the islands, and it resulted in a brief but intense military engagement. The United Kingdom ultimately retained control of the Falklands after a decisive victory.

23. Answers will vary. The Antarctic Treaty, signed in 1959 and entering into force in 1961, is an international agreement that establishes Antarctica as a scientific preserve, bans military activity on the continent, and promotes international scientific cooperation. The treaty, signed by twelve countries initially and now including 54 parties, is significant for international relations because it ensures that Antarctica remains a zone of peace and scientific inquiry, free from territorial disputes and resource exploitation. It is particularly important in light of conflicts because it represents a successful example of global cooperation, setting aside national interests for the common good. By preventing military activities and suspending territorial claims, the treaty helps to mitigate potential conflicts and fosters a spirit of collaboration among nations. December 1, 1959.

24. Answers will vary. Leah was angry and abrupt with Jack about being found. She wanted to be alone possibly to process and let her emotions out where no one could see.

25. *"What part of 'I hate this place' are you not gettin'?"* She doesn't want to stay in Grytviken.

26. Scott landed on the New Zealand side of Antarctica in the Ross Sea, while Shackleton was to land on the South American side in the Weddell Sea. Scott's' goal was to reach the South Pole and return to where he started. Shackleton was to cross the entire continent and arrive where Scott's base was located in the Ross Sea.
Scott crossed using ponies, dogs and motor sledges. All perished or broke down and Scott and his men man-hauled their supplies to survive.
Shackleton was to use dogs and motor sledges but never had the chance due to their failure to reach the shore.

27. Leah is provoking Jack to be jealous. Her response was: *"And you want me to stay here and wait for you!? And you wanna work for them?! No thanks!"* She is pointing out the hypocrisy of Jack's statement.

28. **Illumination:** Whale oil was the best way to get light at night in the 19th century. **Lubrication:** Whale oil was used to lubricate guns, watches, clocks, sewing machines, and typewriters. **Soap production:** Whale oil was used to produce soap from the 16th century through the 19th century.

29. A modern substitute for whale oil is petroleum-based oil, such as mineral oil. Like whale oil, mineral oil is used as a lubricant, in cosmetics, and in industrial applications. However, mineral oil is more stable and has a longer shelf life than whale oil, which can become rancid. Mineral oil is also more readily available and cost-effective, given the large-scale extraction and refinement of petroleum. Unlike whale oil, which required the hunting of whales, mineral oil is derived from crude oil, making it a more sustainable and ethical option in today's context. This shift not only protects whale populations but also ensures a more consistent and versatile supply of the oil for various uses.

30. November 16, 1904. Grytviken, once a bustling whaling station on the island of South Georgia, is no longer active in whaling. The station, which operated from 1904 until the 1960s, has been transformed into a museum and heritage site. Several factors have contributed to Grytviken's current status. First, international regulations such as the International Whaling Commission's (IWC) moratorium on commercial whaling, established in 1986, played a significant role in ending whaling activities. This moratorium was driven by environmental concerns over the declining populations of whale species due to overhunting.
Second, growing environmental awareness and conservation efforts have further pressured countries and companies to cease whaling activities. South Georgia has been designated as a protected area, with the South Georgia and the South

Sandwich Islands Marine Protected Area established to preserve the region's unique ecosystem.

Lastly, the shift in public opinion against whaling, combined with the development of alternative resources and technologies, reduced the demand for whale products. These factors collectively contributed to Grytviken's transformation from a whaling hub to a site of historical and environmental significance, reflecting broader global trends towards conservation and sustainable practices.

31. In the early 20th century, whalers utilized various parts of whales for multiple economic and practical purposes:

Blubber: The blubber was rendered into whale oil through a process called "trying out." This oil was a valuable commodity used for lighting lamps, as a lubricant, and in the production of soap, margarine, and cosmetics. Whale oil was especially prized for its high quality and versatility before the widespread availability of petroleum products.

Meat: While not as widely consumed in Western countries, whale meat was a significant source of protein in some cultures, notably in Japan and Norway. It was used for human consumption and, in some cases, as animal feed. The meat was often salted, smoked, or canned for preservation.

Bones: Whale bones were processed into fertilizer and animal feed. They were also used to create corsets, buggy whips, and other items requiring strong yet flexible materials. Baleen, a specific type of whale bone from baleen whales, was used in fashion for corset stays, skirt hoops, and other clothing accessories due to its flexibility and strength.

Viscera: The internal organs and other by-products, such as blood and intestines, were often used to produce various products. For example, spermaceti, a waxy substance found in the head of sperm whales, was used to make high-quality candles, ointments, and industrial lubricants. Other viscera were sometimes used to produce gelatin and other food additives or were rendered into oils for different industrial purposes.

These uses made whaling a highly profitable industry, as nearly every part of the whale was valuable. This comprehensive utilization of whale products drove the demand for whaling, leading to overexploitation and significant declines in whale populations, eventually prompting the need for international conservation efforts and regulations.

32. Answers may vary. Under United States law, all species of whales are protected by two federal laws, the 1972 Marine Mammal Protection Act and the Endangered Species Act. International efforts to protect whales include several key conservation measures and treaties:

International Whaling Commission (IWC): Established in 1946, the IWC regulates whaling activities to ensure sustainable whale populations. In 1986, the IWC implemented a moratorium on commercial whaling, which remains in effect, though some countries continue whaling under objections or as part of scientific research.

Convention on International Trade in Endangered Species of Wild Fauna and Flora (CITES): Regulates the international trade of whale products to prevent exploitation. Many whale species are listed under CITES Appendix I, which includes species threatened with extinction, thereby prohibiting international trade.

Marine Protected Areas (MPAs): Various MPAs have been established to protect whale habitats. For example, the Southern Ocean around Antarctica is protected under the Antarctic Treaty System, which includes measures to conserve marine life, including whales.

Convention on the Conservation of Migratory Species of Wild Animals (CMS): The CMS works to conserve migratory species, including whales, across their range. It promotes international cooperation and agreements to protect these species and their habitats.

33. Leah thought the expedition was foolishness. Jack leaving her creates a sense of hopelessness and abandonment within her.

34. The Southern Lights (Aurora Australis) and the Northern Lights (Aurora Borealis) are natural light displays predominantly seen near the Earth's polar regions.

Cause: Both the Southern and Northern Lights are caused by the interaction of solar wind—charged particles emitted by the sun—with the Earth's magnetosphere. When these particles collide with gases in the Earth's atmosphere, such as oxygen and nitrogen, they emit light.

Colors: The colors observed in the auroras depend on the type of gas involved and the altitude of the interaction. Oxygen at higher altitudes can produce red and green lights, while nitrogen can result in blue and purplish hues.

Why They Are Visible at the Poles

Magnetic Field: The Earth's magnetic field directs charged solar particles towards the polar regions. The magnetic field lines converge at the poles, guiding these particles into the atmosphere more efficiently there than at lower latitudes.

Geomagnetic Activity: Auroras are most commonly seen in regions known as auroral ovals, centered around the magnetic poles. The increased geomagnetic activity near the poles ensures more frequent and intense displays of auroras.

35. Argentina.

36. Stowaway.

37. Answers may vary. Leah is looking for a fresh start away from whaling, Jack wants to spend time with his brother one day, and Perce is looking for a way home.

38. He received nearly five thousand applications. Twenty-nine men were chosen.

39. Ernest Shackleton faced significant criticisms and skepticism regarding his plans for the *Endurance* expedition:

Winston Churchill: *"Enough life and money has been spent on this sterile quest. The Pole has already been discovered. What is the use of another expedition?"*

Doubts Over Feasibility: Many experts and potential sponsors questioned the feasibility of Shackleton's goal, citing the extreme challenges posed by Antarctica's harsh climate and the vast, uncharted terrain. Critics argued that the technological and logistical limitations of the early 20th century made such an ambitious crossing nearly impossible.

    A. **Financial and Logistical Concerns**: Some skeptics were concerned about the substantial costs and risks associated with the expedition. There were debates over whether the financial investment was justified, especially in light of the high costs of provisioning, the vessel's design, and the support needed for a journey of such magnitude.

    B. **Public Skepticism and Media Coverage**: The media, while often fascinated by Shackleton's daring vision, also published critical views, highlighting the potential dangers and the improbability of success. Newspapers and magazines frequently debated the wisdom of Shackleton's plans, sometimes portraying him as overly ambitious or reckless.

    C. **Expert Opinions and Professional Reactions:** Many seasoned explorers and scientific communities were skeptical of Shackleton's approach. Figures in the field of polar exploration, such as Robert Falcon Scott and Roald Amundsen, had different strategies and goals, leading to a range of opinions on Shackleton's methods and objectives. Some saw Shackleton's focus on a trans-Antarctic crossing as overly ambitious, given the known challenges and previous failures.

    D. **Shackleton's Response to Criticism:** Shackleton, undeterred by the criticisms, remained resolute in his vision. He emphasized the scientific and exploratory value of the journey, promoting the expedition's potential contributions to geographic and scientific knowledge. His charisma, determination, and ability to communicate the adventure's grandeur helped rally support and maintain morale among his team and sponsors.

    E. In summary, while Shackleton's plans were met with significant skepticism and criticism from various quarters, his unwavering commitment and strategic adjustments ultimately underscored his legendary status as an explorer, making the *Endurance* expedition one of the most remarkable stories of Antarctic exploration.

40. 4 August 1914. See also timeline.

41. They offered to cancel the expedition and join the fight pledging the *Endurance*, all of the supplies,and even their own lives to the war effort. The Admiralty said to proceed with the voyage.

42. Some whalers were purchased by the Royal Navy during World War I for use as auxiliary patrol vessels.

43. Churchill: (Answers may vary)
- Was Britain's Prime Minister twice
- He was a prisoner-of-war in South Africa and escaped.
- He was First Lord of the Admiralty in World War I
- He was an accomplished artist
- He won a Nobel Prize in literature

44. The British Imperial Trans-Antarctic Expedition.

45. Answers may vary. The severe conditions, the isolation, and the dangerous mission; all will test them.

46. A capstan is a vertical-axled rotating machine developed for use on sailing ships to multiply the pulling force of seamen when hauling ropes, cables, and hawsers.

47. Two anchors keep the ship from swing in an arc in strong winds, currents or tidal shift.

48. The ship *Endurance* was built in 1912 at the Framnæs shipyard in Sandefjord, Norway, using a combination of strong and durable materials. The hull was primarily constructed of oak, known for its strength, and reinforced with greenheart, one of the hardest woods, for the frames and beams. Pine was used for the decking to balance strength and weight. Additionally, iron and steel reinforcements were strategically placed in the bow and stern to resist ice pressure, and the hull featured double planking for extra durability.
These construction choices were crucial for the expedition, providing the strength and durability needed to navigate the harsh Antarctic conditions. The reinforced bow and stern, along with the flexible wooden structure, allowed *Endurance* to resist the crushing forces of the ice for as long as possible. This robust construction delayed the ship's ultimate fate, giving Shackleton and his crew crucial time to prepare for survival and eventual rescue. The materials and design of *Endurance* exemplified the shipbuilding expertise of the era and were pivotal in supporting Shackleton's ambitious and perilous journey.

49. **The Heroic Age of Polar Exploration** coincided with the Industrial Age because the period's technological advancements made such ambitious expeditions feasible. Innovations like steam-powered ships, improved shipbuilding materials, and enhanced navigation tools significantly increased the safety and efficiency of polar voyages. Developments in communication, such as wireless telegraphy, allowed for better coordination and support. Additionally, advances in clothing, food preservation, and medical supplies improved the survival rates and endurance of explorers in extreme conditions. **These technological breakthroughs provided the necessary tools and infrastructure to undertake and support the challenging and perilous missions to the Earth's polar regions, marking a significant era in the history of exploration.**

50. December 5, 1914. Check timeline on page 37.

51. *Finish the course! We're to follow through with our pledge to earn the trust of men! Ay, You'll have to live with your decisions-good or bad- but its better to sacrifice for the good of others...Things seem to work out better that way...*

52. Answers may vary. To endure would be to "finish the course;" to keep at it until success or fate turns the task too difficult or impossible to complete.

Chapter 2 | The Measure of a Man

1. Fear of heights. Fear impacts decision-making by causing hesitation, second-guessing, and sometimes even paralysis, as individuals may struggle to make choices under the weight

of potential consequences. Within the crew, fear can strain relationships, leading to misunderstandings, conflicts, and a lack of trust. It can also foster a sense of solidarity as crew members band together to face common threats.

2. Marlow is to blame, as his anger and impatience almost killed them both or injured Shackleton. In isolated and high-stress environments like those faced by the *Endurance* crew, tensions can run high, contributing to such conflicts. The consequences of such incidents in these settings can be severe, as they can undermine trust and morale among the crew, potentially jeopardizing the entire mission.

3. **See map.**

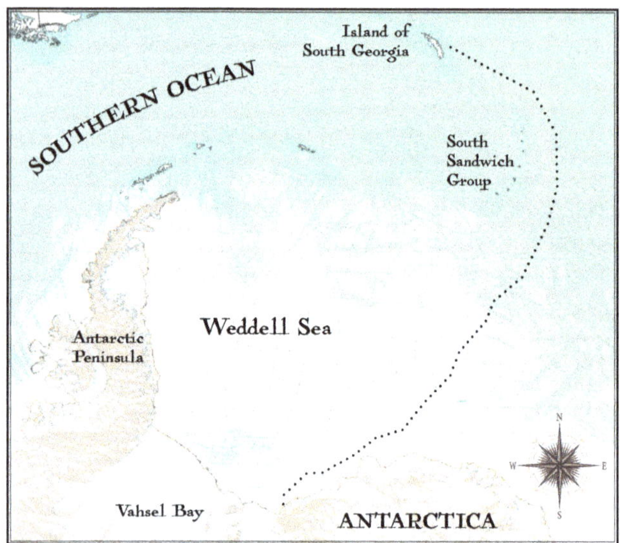

4. Three possible European explorers:
   A. **Capt. James Cook**- Was a British explorer, cartographer and naval officer famous for his three voyages between 1768 and 1779 in the Pacific Ocean and to New Zealand and Australia in particular.
   B. **Christopher Columbus**- Was a navigator, colonizer, and explorer from Genoa, Italy, whose voyages across the Atlantic Ocean led to general European awareness of the American continents in the Western Hemisphere
   C. **Ferdinand Magellan**- In 1519, this Portuguese explorer, with the support of Spain, led the first European voyage to circumnavigate the globe.

5. Three times.
   "My first experience ended in failure... On Captain Scott's Discovery Expedition, I was sent home on a relief ship, debilitated. Then, another chance came in 1907...Sadly, we fell 97 miles short of the South Pole and nearly died on the journey back."

6. **Roald Amundsen.** Norway. December 14th, 1911; See page 37.

7. He was experienced and well equipped. Earlier in his career, Amundsen also explored the northern Arctic regions and was the first person to successfully navigate the Northwest Passage by boat. His voyage lasted from 1903 to 1906. During his northern arctic explorations he stopped at a harbor on King William Island. Members of a local Inuit community taught him how to drive dogs and the skills needed for surviving arctic weather. He applied these skills during his explorations in Antarctica. He used 52 dogs and four expert skiers during his expedition to the South Pole.

8. Scott used very different methods to reach the South Pole. He used a combination of dogs, ponies and motor sledges. The motor sledges broke down and the ponies did not survive; it was necessary for Scott's team to man-haul their supplies. They did not survive.

9. The Trans Continental Party was to land at Vahsel Bay, establish winter shelter, lay out supply depots, then leave that next summer to cross the continent.

10. The Ross Sea Party was to land on the opposite side of Antarctica, then begin to lay food and supply depots at regular intervals all the way to the meeting point of the two parties. This food would allow Shackleton and his team to survive the rest of the 900+ mile trek to the Ross Sea base.

11. **Sled, toboggan, dogsled, sleigh.** Sleds played a crucial role in Antarctic expeditions, serving as the primary means for transporting supplies, equipment, and sometimes even personnel across the harsh, icy terrain. They enabled explorers to carry heavy loads over long distances, essential for survival and success in such remote and unforgiving environments. The use of dog sleds, in particular, provided both speed and efficiency, capitalizing on the strength and *Endurance* of sled dogs. Sleds were fundamental to the logistics of polar travel, allowing expeditions to explore deeper into the continent, conduct scientific research, and achieve significant milestones in the history of exploration..

12. Use a board to separate them and call for help.

13. Frank Wild or Shackleton would likely advise Jack and Perce to remain calm and composed in the face of bullying, emphasizing the importance of maintaining unity and morale within the crew. They might suggest addressing the issue directly and respectfully with Marlow, possibly mediated by a senior member, to resolve the conflict. Furthermore, they would likely encourage Jack to focus on the larger mission and his duties, reminding him of the strength and resilience required to endure the challenges of their expedition. They could also offer personal support and mentorship, reinforcing the importance of solidarity and respect among the crew.

14. Death, Shackleton's conscience and dread, the voice of spiritual darkness, etc.

15. Answers will vary. Jack prays for help, and Shackleton comforts himself by remembering his experience and preparation.

16. The left side of the boat toward the front. Starboard bow.

17. December 7, 1914. See timeline for date.

18. December 17, 1912. See timeline for date.

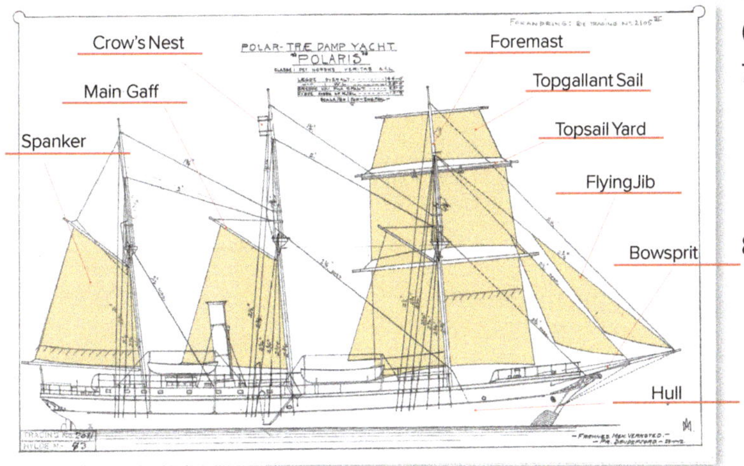

19. **See ship blueprint above for correct entries.**

20. A *barquentine-rigged ship* is a sailing ship of three or more masts with a square rigged foremast and fore-and-aft rigged main, mizzen and any other masts.

21. Any area of sea ice (formed by freezing of seawater) that is not land-fast; it is mobile by virtue of not being attached to the shoreline or something else.

22. They would run out of fuel; they could damage the engines.

23. A growler is a piece of ice that breaks off from icebergs, glaciers (this process is called "calving"), and shelf ice. It is floating in open water, and might be an obstacle for small boats. According to NOAA Ocean Service, a growler is a piece of ice less than 1 meter high above sea level, and less than 5 meters long.

24. The massive icebergs are formed by ice breaking off from the continental ice shelf.

25. Answers will vary depending on the animal students choose. Example: Penguins are well adapted to the cold because of their thick blubber layer and their waterproof feathers. They can also drink saltwater. Petrels have waterproof feathers to keep the icy water from touching their skin as well as a thick undercoat to retain warmth. In the winter, they migrate farther north.

Chapter 3 | The Sea of Decision

1. He was a whaler. He was too old. She loved Jack.

2. Animasl found only in Antarctica:

    A. Emperor penguins
    B. Leopard seal
    C. Adélie penguins
    D. Pink-faced Sheathbill

3. Answers will vary and can be as simple or detailed as students have time, but they could include ideas like a dangerous build-up of carbon dioxide in the ocean and atmosphere, a large die-off of animals that depend on krill for food, the phytoplankton that krill eat could reproduce at an accelerated rate and create toxins in the water.

4. January 10, 1915. See timeline on page 37 for date.

5. Approximately 600 miles.

6. Approximately 200-300 miles.

7. Worsley joined the New Zealand Shipping Company in 1888. He served aboard several vessels running trade routes between New Zealand, England and the South Pacific. While on South Pacific service, he was known for his ability to navigate to tiny, remote islands.

8. Navigating through pack ice and sailing through a coral reef both present significant dangers but in different ways. Pack ice can trap and crush ships, making it difficult to move forward or retreat, and it often forms unpredictably, posing a constant threat to the vessel's hull. On the other hand, sailing through a coral reef requires careful navigation to avoid running aground on sharp, hidden coral formations, which can tear open a ship's hull and cause severe damage or sinking. While pack ice primarily poses a danger due to its crushing force and vast, shifting nature, coral reefs present hazards due to their fixed, jagged structures and the precise navigation they demand. Both environments require vigilance and skill to navigate safely.

9. The pack ice moved because of winds or currents to collide with each other.

10. To heave astern means to pull or move a ship backward, often using a capstan, windlass, or other mechanical means to haul the vessel in reverse. This maneuver is typically employed to free the ship from ice or other obstacles, or to reposition it in a more favorable direction.

11. Used to secure the ship to an ice flow to weather storms. Used to provide relief for the crew to stretch their legs and exercise.

12. The capstan works in tandem with the propeller, adding much needed backward force to free the ship from the vice-like grip of the ice. The crew of the *Endurance* needed ice anchors and a capstan in addition to the engine because the engine alone was not powerful enough to escape the grip of the ice floes. Ice anchors provided secure points to pull the ship, while the capstan allowed the crew to manually haul the vessel in combination with the engine's efforts. This multifaceted approach was necessary to extract the ship from the challenging and dangerous predicament.

13. European whalers have moved from the Arctic regions to the Southern Ocean primarily due to the depletion of whale populations in the Arctic caused by extensive hunting. The Southern Ocean, with its rich whale populations, provided a lucrative alternative. Additionally, advancements in shipbuilding and navigation made it possible for whalers to venture into these previously inaccessible southern waters.

14. A suffragette was a member of an activist women's organization in the early 20th century who, under the banner "Votes for Women", fought for the right to vote in public elections in the United Kingdom. They used art, debate, propaganda, and attack on property including window smashing and arson to fight for female suffrage.

15. Cinderella.

16. In both cases, the Grim Reaper plays on their doubts and fears and makes them question their decisions. But Leah had someone to help her–Mrs. Cotburn.

17. The 1904–1905 Welsh revival was the largest Christian revival in Wales during the 20th century. It was one of the most dramatic in terms of its effect on the population, and triggered revivals in several other countries. The movement kept the churches of Wales filled for many years to come. Meanwhile, the Awakening swept the rest of Britain, Scandinavia, parts of Europe, North America, the mission fields of India and the Orient, Africa and Latin America. The Welsh revival has been traced as the root of the megachurches in the present era.

18. Her own life was burdened with prejudices because of her race. That she is grateful for what she has.

19. Fill in the blanks:"*God knows your battle with the* **whalers.** *He knows your* **heart***! You're* **golden** *in His eyes...He has told me He has* **plans** *for you... a* **hope** *and a* **future***...Don't give up! Everything's gonna be made new again..."*

20. Really wanting to know how to help him out.

21. *"It's yer first time on a ship...It's not easy!"* And *"Easy mate! It'll get better... You'll see!"*

22. Answers will vary. Because it would make their provisions last longer; because fresh food is healthier.

23. By knowing the details, Shackleton can address the root causes, mediate effectively, and maintain discipline and morale. This transparency ensures that decisions are based on accurate information, promoting trust and respect within the team. It also enables the leader to provide appropriate support and guidance, preventing further escalation and fostering a cooperative and harmonious environment

24. *"After what happen'd to me in China, the kid better stay far away from me..."*

25. 1918.

26. Answers will vary. Ex. Infections and disease, hot and cold temperatures, issues like trench foot, artillery fire, rats, boredom, mental health issues.

27. Answers will vary. Encourage the student to follow through with this question.

28. Jack misses his older brother and feels insecure on how to best handle all of his stress.

29. Apollyon, Abaddon.

30. Answers will vary. Find his way to God. Find an inner strength within. Find that strength from God to endure.

31. Stress, anxiety, and major life changes often manifest in vivid or recurring dreams, while positive experiences can lead to pleasant dreams. Essentially, dreams can reflect our subconscious attempts to understand and cope with our waking life experiences.

32. Answers will vary. His brother had hope in death, but he doesn't; his brother's soul was safe, but his isn't.

33. Find the title and author/source of each quote shown here:

1. *For Whom the Bell Tolls.* Author: John Donne
2. Psalm 91:5 Source: Holy Bible
3. Proverbs 29:25 Source: Holy Bible

34. 62° F below freezing (32° F). 34.4° C below 0°.

Book Two, The Beckoning Shore
Prologue

1. In earlier days, snow and ice was shoveled into large tanks and heated to melt into water. At Australia's Casey and Mawson research stations in Antarctica, water is produced primarily by melting snow with an electrically heated 'melt bell', in a cavern underneath the ice.

2. He will soon face grave dangers to the ship and crew.

3. As the iceberg drifted through the Weddell Sea, it eventually encountered a submerged ridge or shallow region, causing it to become stuck. This grounding was a result of the iceberg's large volume and the interaction with the sea floor, which prevented it from continuing its movement through the water.

4. 1,800 ft.

5. The currents pulled the ship away from colliding with the berg.

6. 40 degrees.

7. 120 degrees.

8. GPS-Global Positioning System.

9. In the chance their navigational instruments are broken or destroyed.

10. Label the parts of this sextant: **See drawing.**

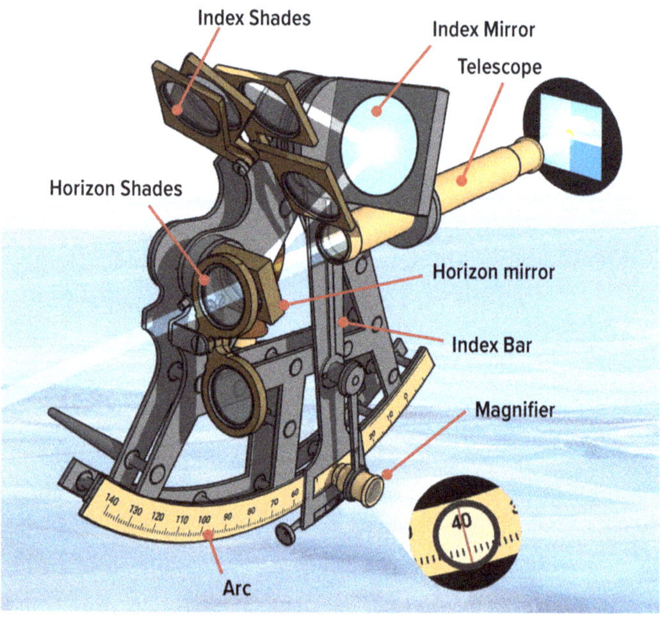

Chapter 1 | The Keep

11. During the summer at the poles, the Sun moves around the horizon in a circle and is visible nearly 24 hours a day due to the tilt of the Earth's axis. The Earth's axial tilt of

approximately 23.5 degrees causes one pole to be tilted towards the Sun, resulting in continuous daylight for about six months. This phenomenon is known as the Midnight Sun..

12. The dogs grow very thick coats that trap the heat near the skin. They can still freeze to death if there is no food to supply heat energy through metabolism.

13. **Hypothermia.** Abnormally low body temperature can make you sleepy, confused, and clumsy. Because it happens gradually and affects your thinking, you may not realize you need help.

14. Because it doesn't get colder than 32 degrees under the snow.

15. In the fall of 1915. Sept 25-Oct. 8, 1915 check timeline on page 37.

16. The **Just War Theory** is a largely Christian philosophy that attempts to reconcile three things: taking human life is seriously wrong. Nations have a duty to defend their citizens, and defend justice. Protecting innocent human life and defending important moral values sometimes requires willingness to use force.

17. The Battle of Loos took place from Sept. 25 to Oct. 8, 1915 in France on the Western Front, during World War I. It was the biggest British attack of 1915, the first time that the British used poison gas and the first mass engagement of New Army units. Despite improved methods, more ammunition, better equipment and gas, the Franco-British attacks were contained by the Germans, except for local losses of ground. The British gas attack failed sufficiently to neutralize the defenders and the artillery bombardment was too short to destroy barbed wire and machine gun nests. German defensive fortifications and tactics could not be overcome by the British who were still assembling a mass army suitable for Western Front conditions. British casualties suffered in the main attack were 48,367 and they suffered 10,880 more in the subsidiary attack, a total of 59,247. German losses in the battle were approximately 26,000.

18. October 27, 1915. Check page 37.

19. Massive currents and collisions of the ice fields in the Weddell Sea caused the ice to increase the pressure on the hull until it broke.

20. A keel is the main structural member and backbone of a ship or boat, running longitudinally along the center of the bottom of the hull from stem to stern.
In sailboats, keels serve two purposes:
    1. As an underwater foil to keep the vessel moving straight while under sail.
    2. As a counterweight to the wind on the sails that causes rolling to the side (heeling).

21. He gave them hope by referring to a rescue hut on Paulet Island. He complimented them on the great work and character they showed throughout the ordeal. He showed confidence that they would survive through trust and hard work.

22. The stove is designed to consume blubber for fuel. Since there is no wood available for fuel to burn for heat, seal fat or blubber is rich in energy, and when prepared, can be used to heat and cook food.

23. The safety and survival of his men were his top concerns. His experience with the Antarctic ice and cold can help guide him to make wise decisions. He had studied the plans for all contingencies a hundred times. He can rely on his strength of mind and experience to push his fears down and determines to create a strategy for them to survive.

Chapter 2 | The Frozen Sea

1. The "grim elementary forces": Wind is the main driving force, along with ocean currents. The Coriolis force and sea ice surface tilt have also been invoked. These driving forces induce a state of stress within the drift ice zone. An ice floe converging toward another and pushing against it will generate a state of compression at the boundary between both. If two floes drift sideways past each other while remaining in contact, this will create a state of shear. Shackleton's observation about the ice blocks highlights the immense power and unpredictability of an ice-bound sea. The description of huge blocks of ice being lifted and tossed aside demonstrates the uncontrollable forces at play. Shackleton's sense of helplessness and the acknowledgment that their lives depended on these "grim elementary forces" emphasize the dangerous and precarious nature of their situation, underscoring the vulnerability of humans in such extreme conditions.

2. November 21. 1915. Check this date on page 37.

3. December 23, 1915. Check timeline on page 37.

4. **Fill in the blanks on the map.**

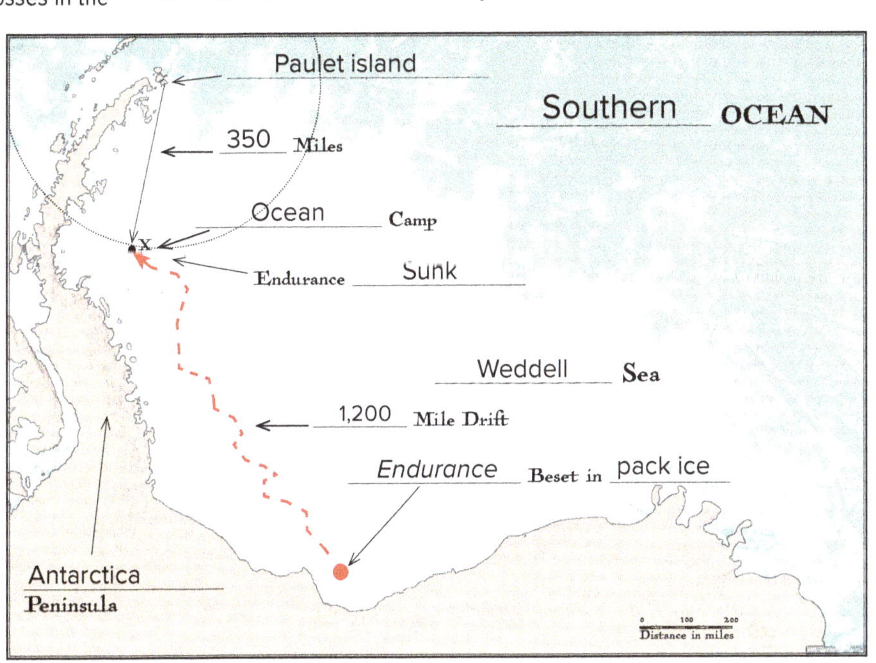

5. A line of piled-up ice that's created when pack ice expands and contracts with temperature changes. Also from pressure exerted on the ice by the force of the wind or tides or movement of the ice by the underlying ocean currents. A section of the ice pack that buckles under the force of two gigantic ice packs pressing together.

6. Boundaries or cracks in the ice sheet that are filled with water. A large fracture within an expanse of sea ice, defining a linear area of open water that can be used for navigation purposes. Leads vary in width from meters to hundreds of meters.

7. The sun and air temperature was sometimes warm enough to melt the ice.

8. Spring.

9. Its very hard and slow work hauling the boats. They believe there is ice all the way to the island even though they have no way of knowing if that's true. Shackleton won't gamble and take that risk for the rest of the men's sake.

10. In case they want to overcome Shackleton with force. To show they will not lose control of the team.

11. They were on a frozen sea. Once the ice breaks up, they will need the boats to survive.

12. The ship's articles says his command is in force until they are disbanded or reach safety.

13. As tempting as it is to do the quick and easy path, understanding the risks involved, it's best to follow Shackleton's lead.

14. The ice is soft and thinning out. Shackleton fears losing a boat. The worst part is the men attached to it would die as they are pulled down to the sea bottom.

15. **December 29, 1915.** Summer. Check the timeline on page 37.

16. The name Patience Camp was appropriate because they endured months of waiting for the ice to break up to launch the boats.

17. The Boss makes the decision to put the dogs down as they will suffer starvation and die.

18. A predator at the top of a food chain, without natural predators of its own.

19. **Leopard seals** (Hydrurga leptonyx) are large marine mammals found in the cold waters surrounding Antarctica. They are known for their distinctive long bodies, large heads, and powerful jaws, which are equipped with sharp, interlocking teeth. Leopard seals have a unique spotted coat, which ranges in color from silver to dark gray, helping them blend into their icy environment.
    They are solitary creatures, often seen alone or in small groups. They are formidable hunters, feeding on a wide variety of prey, including fish, squid, penguins, and even other seals. Their powerful jaws and agile swimming abilities make them adept at catching fast-moving prey. They are particularly known for their skill in hunting penguins, often waiting near ice edges to ambush them as they enter the water. Leopard seals can grow up to 11.5 feet in length and weigh between 800 to 1,300 pounds, with females generally being larger than males. They are vocal animals, producing a range of sounds underwater that are believed to play a role in communication, particularly during the breeding season. Their population is currently stable.

20. Research and find 3 other reported attacks by leopard seals.

    A. In 1985, Canadian-British explorer Gareth Wood was bitten twice on the leg when a leopard seal tried to drag him off the ice and into the sea. His companions managed to save him by repeatedly kicking the animal in the head with the spiked crampons on their boots.

    B. September 2021. Near the dive site Spaniard Rock at Simon's Town, South Africa, three spear-fisherman encountered a leopard seal approximately 400 meters offshore. The seal attacked, disarming them of their flippers and spear guns, and kept harassing the men over the course of half an hour, inflicting multiple bite and puncture wounds.

    C. **In 2003, biologist Kirsty Brown of the British Antarctic Survey was killed by a leopard seal while snorkeling in Antarctica.** Brown and another researcher, Richard Burt, were snorkeling in the water. Burt was snorkeling 15 meters away when the team heard a scream and saw Brown disappear into the water. She was quickly rescued by her team but they were unable to resuscitate her. It was later revealed that the seal had held her underwater for six minutes at a depth of up to 70 meters.

21. Seal blubber.

22. *"This storm should speed up our movement to the sea... the wind direction is pushing us north."*

23. They will reach the open Southern Ocean and the ice will begin to break up.

24. Several dogs had died, and more than a few were sick.

25. A dog is man's **best friend.**

26. Two modern techniques used in rescue operations to locate shipwrecks include satellite imagery and sonar technology. Satellite imagery allows for the observation of large ocean areas, identifying unusual surface patterns that may indicate the presence of a shipwreck. High-resolution satellite images can also track changes over time, helping to locate debris fields. Sonar technology, particularly multi-beam and side-scan sonar, is used to create detailed images of the seafloor. These systems emit sound waves that bounce off objects on the ocean floor, providing data that can be used to map out the location and shape of wreckage.

27. Psalm 42:7

28. Ernest Shackleton was criticized for not equipping the *Endurance* expedition with a Marconi wireless telegraph, which could have sent out a distress call to alert rescuers. This technology was relatively new at the time and had the capability to transmit Morse Code signals over long distances. Shackleton's decision not to include this equipment was likely influenced by a combination of factors, including the high cost, the perceived reliability of the ship

and expedition plan, and possibly a lack of awareness about the practical applications and importance of wireless communication in such remote regions.

29. Answers may vary. The apostle Paul was a prisoner of Rome being taken by guard to stand trial before Caesar. They encountered a vicious storm and was shipwrecked on the island of Malta in the Mediterranean Sea. They landed on an occupied island and were treated kindly and with respect. The *Endurance* shipwreck was many hundreds of miles from any help and they were completely icebound.

Chapter 3 | Strangers in Strange Land

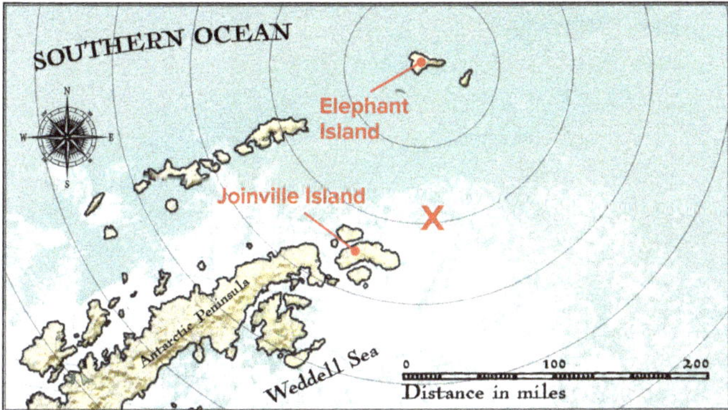

1. On the map, locate Joinville Island and Elephant Island.

2. See location on map. Joinville island is closer.

3. *"It'd be suicide to try to reach that...Ice's too loose to go on foot and not open enough t' launch th' boats..."* It was too difficult and too risky to attempt Joinville Island.

4. The Weddell Gyre is a large, circular ocean current in the Southern Ocean surrounding Antarctica. It moves in a clockwise direction, driven primarily by the Earth's rotation and the prevailing wind patterns. This gyre helps push the pack ice in the Weddell Sea northward. The factors contributing to its formation include the interaction of the Antarctic Circumpolar Current with the Earth's rotation, which generates the rotational movement of the gyre; and the cold, dense water from the Antarctic Ice Sheet, which influences the movement of both the water and the ice.

5. The waves in a fully developed sea outrun the storm that creates them, traveling great distances from the wind source and lengthening and reducing in height in the process. These lower frequency waves are called swell waves. Swells organize into groups smooth and regular in appearance. They are able to travel thousands of miles unchanged in height and period. The longer the wave, the faster it travels. As waves leave a storm area, they tend to sort themselves out with the long ones ahead of the short ones, and the energy is simultaneously spread out over an increasingly larger area.

6. Factors contributing to ice floes breaking apart include changes in temperature, ocean currents, wind patterns, tidal forces, and the mechanical stress from the movement of other ice masses. Warmer temperatures can weaken the ice, while strong currents and winds can push ice floes into each other or against landmasses, causing them to crack and break apart.

7. **April 9, 1916.** Check page 37.

8. *"Through it all, Providence has determined our fate, and now we place our hope in God and in this able crew..."* He gives credit to God and his fellow crew mates.

9. He is concerned they will survive.

10. Answers may vary; Whales, Orcas, Seals, Penguins, Cape Pigeons, Petrels and Fulmars. The crew might have observed several specific species of Antarctic animals, such as emperor penguins, Weddell seals, leopard seals, and various species of albatross and petrels. Additionally, they could have seen krill swarming in the water and possibly even sightings of whales such as orcas or humpbacks feeding nearby.

11. A pelagic bird lives most of its life at sea, only living on land during its mating and nesting season.

12. Research and make a list of 5 facts about Adélie penguins that distinguish them from other penguins.

    1. They are the most widespread species of penguin.
    2. They have a distinct white ring around their eyes.
    3. They're one of only two penguin species that live that far south.
    4. They don't like to jump into the water—they wait to be pushed in.
    5. They're one of the friendliest and most curious species of penguin.

13. White reflects sunlight and keeps the hull cooler, which can help prevent marine growth. Some bottom paints are formulated with biocides or other additives to prevent the growth of marine organisms, such as barnacles, algae, and mollusks.

14. *Orcinus* translates to 'of the kingdom of the dead,' and orca refers to a kind of whale.

15. Dolphin.

16. Orcas can be found in all of the world's oceans, but are most common in colder waters and coastal areas. Some of the best places to see orcas in the wild include: Alaska, Antarctica, Norway, Pacific Northwest, Puget Sound in Seattle, and Galapagos Islands.

17. They are the apex predator in all the world's oceans and seas. They are highly social; some populations are composed of tight-knit family groups (pods) which are the most stable of any animal species. Their sophisticated hunting techniques and vocal behaviors, which are often specific to a particular group and passed across generations, have been described as manifestations of animal culture.

18. The orca lives to an age of 50 to 80 years.

19. 23 to 32 feet and weigh up to 6 tons.

20. Examples: **2020, a subpopulation of orcas began ramming boats and attacking their rudders in waters off the Iberian Peninsula.** The behavior has generally been directed towards slow-moving, medium-sized sailboats in the Strait of Gibraltar

and off the Portuguese, Moroccan and Galician coasts. The novel behavior is thought to have spread between different pods, with over 500 reported interactions from 2020 to 2023. **Winter of 2023-24 in San Diego, California-** A pod of orcas hunted dolphins near to surfers who were riding waves.

21. The lifeboats can only hold **10-12 men** with supplies. Any more, the boat could flounder in the rough ocean and sink, leaving everyone to drown.

22. The crew's drift backward in the Weddell Sea was primarily caused by the strong, shifting sea ice and ocean currents. In the Weddell Sea, the ice floes move in a complex pattern that can carry ships or boats in unintended directions. Additionally, the pack ice's movement, driven by wind and ocean currents, could have pushed the boats away from their intended course, causing the backward drift.

23. They wanted speed and buoyancy in the open ocean.

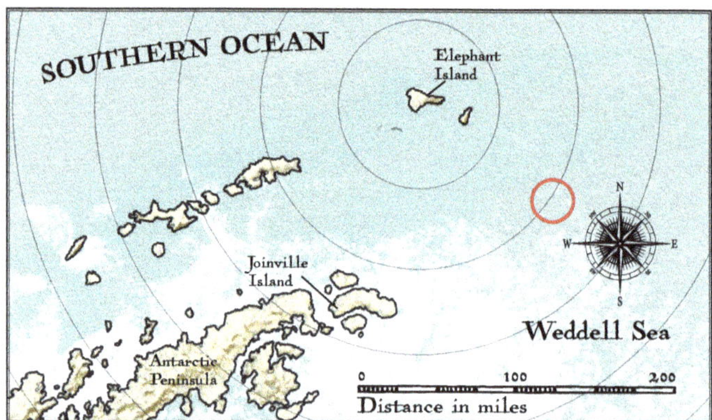

24. **See map above for approximate circle of the boats' location.** Anything east of Elephant Island is good. Shackleton and his crew had to sail west to reach Elephant Island because they had been drifted eastward from their initial position. This drift was caused primarily by the movement of the pack ice and the strong ocean currents in the Weddell Sea. The northern Weddell Sea moves predominantly eastward due to the prevailing winds and the clockwise rotation of the **Weddell Gyre**. This drift pushed the boats off their intended course, requiring them to adjust their navigation to compensate for the displacement.

25. She's writing to *The Times of London,* hoping they will publish her letter and share the horrors of the whaling industry with the world. She may hope that the right people will read the letter and help her end whaling.

26. That the whalers deserve it for what they do to the whales.

27. She reacted in anger and felt justified in doing the misdeed.

28. Answers may vary. It may have hurt her cause because she angered the whalers and her father. Also, there's no one else on the island to see her message except people in the whaling industry. On the other hand, it may have helped her cause because she now has a way off the island.

29. **Greenpeace** is an anti-whaling group founded in 1971 and has had numerous campaigns to stop whaling. **Sea Shepherd** is an international direct-action ocean conservation movement that started in 1977. They rely on

confrontation with whalers and see themselves as the enforcers against whale harvesting. In 2011-12, there were clashes between Sea Shepherd and Japanese whalers off Antarctica. Tear gas and grappling hooks were used against the giant Japanese whaling ships.

30. Strong wind with frozen rain.

31. Blood has salt in it.

32. Drinking seawater for thirst can lead to dehydration because the human body requires more water to expel the excess salt than the seawater provides. This can worsen dehydration and lead to serious health problems such as kidney failure and eventually death.

33. When sea ice is formed, the salt content is significantly reduced compared to the surrounding seawater. Most of the salt is expelled during the freezing process, creating brine pockets that eventually drain out. As a result, the newly formed sea ice has a much lower salinity. However, freshly formed sea ice is still not entirely free of salt and is not immediately safe to drink. Over time, the salt content continues to decrease, making the older, multi-year sea ice relatively safer for consumption, but it is still recommended to desalinate it further before drinking.

34. A narrow piece of land that projects from a coastline into the sea.

35. April 16, 1916. Check page 37. 497 days

36. They praise him, saying he's amazing. Earlier, they doubted him, questioned him, and even tried to break up the crew in a mutiny against him.

37. **See map.**

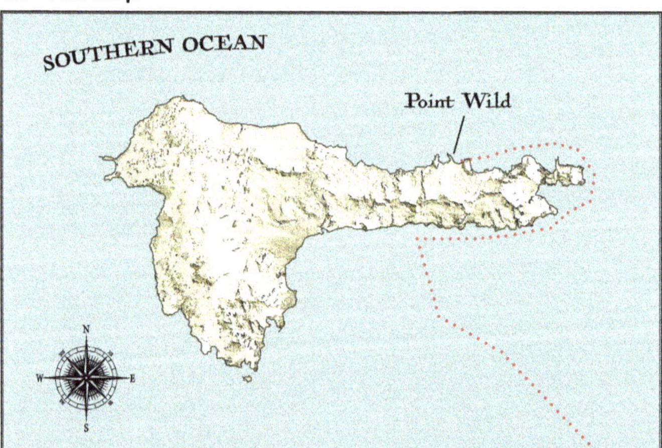

Chapter 4 | The Beckoning Shore

1. He is a veteran of war and the horrors of combat haunt him.

2. Soldiers marching or fighting on foot, or foot soldiers.

3. They now have steel helmets for better head protection. Air bursts of artillery shells would send steel shards shooting down on the soldiers in the trenches. Plus, machine guns were taking a toll.

4. Big guns that fire exploding shells over long distance to destroy the enemy positions.

5. To destroy the British artillery so they can't fire on the advancing Germans.

6. Mortars are small artillery weapons that are very mobile and can be carried by soldiers to the front lines. The shells travel in a high arc and can be adjusted precisely to land and explode on a specific target.

7. 50 to 250 yards apart.

8. The land between was called "No Man's Land".

9. Hyperbole is an exaggerated statement meant to make a point. The war has revealed so much evil in the world that it would seem better to have never been born into it.

10. War in Afghanistan, Iraq, Israel/Gaza, Ukraine, etc.

11. They are far from shipping lanes with no hope of rescue.

12. A boat will be outfitted and 5 men will sail to South Georgia to get help for the rest of the men.

13. When winter sets in, they could be blocked or iced in on their voyage and lost forever. Storms are more frequent and severe. It's dark most of the time.

14. Answers may vary. For more than four months, from April 24 to August 30, 1916, during the Antarctic winter, Wild and his crew waited on Elephant Island, surviving on a diet of seal, penguin and seaweed. They built makeshift huts by resting their two remaining lifeboats upside down on rocks. To combat the perpetual darkness, they made lamps out of sardine tins, used surgical bandages for wicks, and burned seal blubber oil.

15. April 24, 1916. Check timeline on page 37.

16. See map. It is approximately **800** miles.

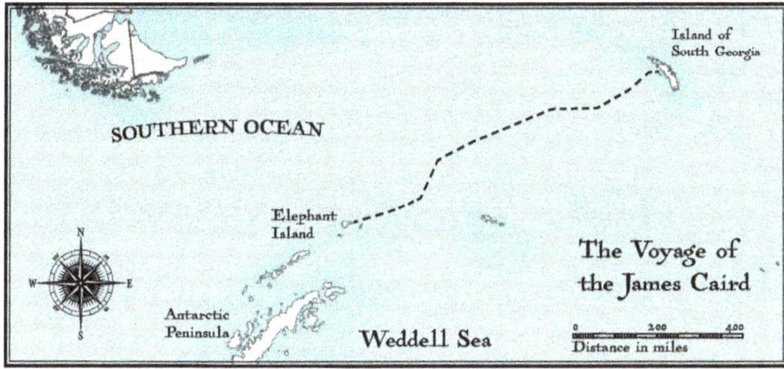

17. Shanties helped sailors and fishermen relieve boredom, and they helped the crew coordinate their movements around the ship as they work.

18. Writing a sea shanty is a creative exercise, so have fun!

19. He thought the storm was ending.

20. A lot of speed to get over and through the wave.

21. Treacherous reefs and high cliffs made landing impossible.

22. Overnight to the next day. **May 10, 1916.** See page 37.

23. They will cross the mountains to get help.

24. Shackleton and his companions faced numerous dangers during their trek through the mountains. They encountered extreme weather conditions, including severe cold, strong winds, and snowstorms, which posed risks of frostbite, hypothermia, and disorientation. The treacherous terrain, characterized by steep, icy, and unstable slopes, increased the likelihood of avalanches, falls, and injuries. Additionally, poor visibility from fog or blizzards could hinder navigation, raising the risk of getting lost. They also had to contend with limited food and water supplies, which could lead to dehydration and starvation, and the physical exhaustion from the arduous journey, which could impair their ability to make sound decisions. These factors combined to create a perilous situation that required resilience and careful planning to survive.

25. She will be writing about the industry her family supports. This would be a direct attack on her father's business also, so they may feel betrayed by her.

26. Answers will vary. **Crampons:** These are metal spikes that attach to the bottom of boots to provide traction on ice. They come in various designs, such as semi-rigid with step-in systems or flexible ones with toe straps, making them suitable for different activities, from technical climbing to general winter hiking. The spikes dig into the ice, offering stability and grip. **Ice Axes:** Essential for ice climbing, ice axes are used to secure climbers to the ice and aid in pulling themselves up. Technical ice axes have curved shafts to support weight better and can also be used for self-arrest in case of a slip

27. Match the words to their meaning by drawing a line connecting them:

clipper — supervises and directs other workers

gale — taking in or rolling up a sail to reduce the area exposed to the wind

foreman — merchant ship that plied global routes and ferried cargo and passengers

aloft — a strong wind

reef — at, on, or to the masthead or the higher rigging

28. Marlow was having an argument with the foreman over the rigging and the shipmate next to him lost his grip and fell into the sea.

29. Clippers were built in Europe and the US, and junks were built in China and other parts of Asia. Clippers are no longer being built, but junks are. Junks have been around hundreds of years longer than clippers. Freighters are much larger than clippers and junks, designed to carry cargo long distances.

30. The Suez Canal an artificial sea-level waterway in Egypt, connecting the Mediterranean Sea to the Red Sea through the Isthmus of Suez and dividing Africa and Asia (and by extension, the Sinai Peninsula from the rest of Egypt). The 193.30-kilometer-long (120.11 mi) canal is a key trade route between Europe and Asia. The canal officially opened on November 17, 1869. It offers vessels a direct route between the North Atlantic and northern Indian oceans via the Mediterranean Sea and the Red Sea, avoiding the South Atlantic and southern Indian oceans. It reduces the journey from the Arabian Sea to London by approximately 8,900 kilometers (5,500 mi).

31. **See map.**

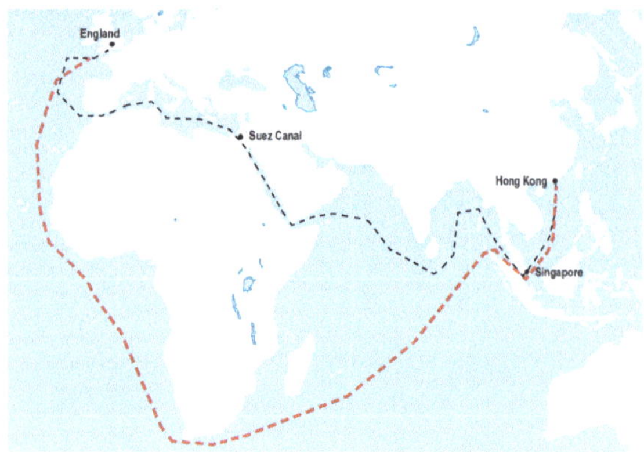

32. May 20, 1916 they arrived in Stromness. Check page 37.

33. 20 miles/32 km.

34. Exercise for student to create a map of the neighborhood they live.

35. *"The protective care of God or of nature as a spiritual power."* -Dictionary.

36. Leah will sail to Norway then to England.

37. A telegraph machine is a device used for sending and receiving messages over long distances through electrical signals transmitted via wires. Invented in the early 19th century by Samuel Morse and Alfred Vail, the telegraph revolutionized communication by allowing instant transmission of information,. The telegraph played a crucial role in various aspects of society, including commerce, journalism, and military operations. Its use declined with the advent of more advanced technologies like the telephone and the internet, but its impact on the development of modern communication systems is significant.

38. Morse Code is a method of encoding text characters through sequences of short-signal dots and long-signal dashes, representing letters, numbers, and punctuation. Despite being developed in the 1830s, Morse Code is still used today in specialized fields such as amateur radio, aviation, and maritime communication, mainly as a backup method for transmitting information when other communication systems fail.

39. *Endurance.*

40. Exercise: send a one-word Morse Code message.

41. Despite her secret plan to go to England, Leah decides to return to Grytviken upon hearing the news about Jack. This decision indicates that her love for Jack far outweighs her previous plans; her emotional connection and sense of responsibility toward him are stronger than her desire to leave for England. Her immediate decision to leave the ship and return to Grytviken shows that her priority is to be with Jack, regardless of the disruption to her original plans.

42. Answers may vary. Jack and Marlow might have attempted to repair the lifeboat and sail to a whaling station or another inhabited area. They could have tried to signal passing ships using mirrors, fires, or makeshift signals. Constructing a more substantial shelter and rationing supplies would have been crucial for survival while awaiting a potential rescue.

Additionally, they might have explored other parts of South Georgia for alternative routes or resources and left clear signs indicating their presence and direction of travel for any rescue parties. Ultimately, their survival would have depended on their ability to endure the harsh environment and wait for rescue.

43. A boat that guides ships into and out of ports.

44. It's Spanish for "Captain! Land in sight!"

45. August 30, 1916 Check timeline on page 37.

46. *Is everyone safe?*

47. The expedition returned to England in piecemeal fashion, at a critical stage in the war, without any civic receptions. When Shackleton himself finally arrived in England on May 29, 1917, after a short American lecture tour, his return was barely noticed or covered by the press.

48. Answers may vary. They represent the reader's point of view; they're useful for helping us understand what's happening in the story, or gives clarity to the story.

49. Shackleton took part in how many Antarctic expeditions? **4**

50. The date of his death? **January 5, 1922**

51. Where is he buried? **Grytviken, South Georgia.**

52. At the time of his death, he was deeply in **debt**.

53. Wild joined **5** expeditions to Antarctica.

54. He was awarded the **Polar Medal** with four bars, one of only two men to be so honored.

55. He was buried in 2011 next to Shackleton in South Georgia.

56. He was **captain** of the *Endurance*.

57. Worsley's expert **navigational** skills was responsible for the survival of the entire expedition party.

58. In 1922, he sailed with **Shackleton** on his final Antarctic expedition.

59. During Scott's 1913 Terra Nova Expedition where Scott and his party **perished**, Crean hiked **35** miles alone across the ice to save the life of Edward Evans.

60. How many Antarctic expeditions did Crean go on? **3**

61. Perce came on board the *Endurance* as a **stowaway**.

62. He suffered **frostbite** on Elephant Island and lost his **left foot** to amputation.

63. He received the Bronze **Polar** Medal for his service.

Epilogue

64. The *Endurance*22 Expedition.

65. Answers may vary. The enormity of finding a ship nearly two miles beneath the ocean, requires sophisticated location equipment and expert knowledge.

66. 10,000 feet below

67. It will remain undisturbed. It will be illegal and unethical to disturb the resting place of the *Endurance*.

68. March 5, 2022. Check timeline on page 37.